A Stolen Life

A Stolen Life

JANE LOUISE CURRY

MARGARET K. MCELDERRY BOOKS

ALSO BY JANE LOUISE CURRY:

The Christmas Knight
illustrated by DyAnne DiSalvo-Ryan

Back in the Beforetime: Tales of the California Indians
illustrated by James Watts

Moon Window

Dark Shade

Turtle Island: Tales of the Algonquian Nations
illustrated by James Watts

(MARGARET K. MCELDERRY BOOKS)

Margaret K. McElderry Books
An imprint of Simon & Schuster Children's Publishing Division
1230 Avenue of the Americas
New York, New York 10020

Book design by Ann Bobco
The text of this book was set in New Caledonia.
Printed in the United States of America
10 9 8 7 6 5 4 3 2 1
Library of Congress Cataloging-in-Publication Data
Curry, Jane Louise.
A Stolen Life / by Jane Louise Curry. p. cm.
Summary: In 1758 in Scotland, teenaged Jamesina MacKensie finds her courage and resolution severely tested when she is abducted by "spiriters" and, after a harrowing voyage, sold as a bond slave to a Virginia planter.
ISBN 0-689-82932-9
[1. Indentured servants—Fiction. 2. Scotland—History—18th century—Fiction.
3. Virginia—History—Colonial period, 1600-1775—Fiction.] I. Title.
PZ7.C936St 1999 [Fic]—dc21 98-51103

For Zoe

Scotland

1758

1

JAMESINA AWOKE TO THE SOUND OF VOICES IN THE LOWER house. Pushing the covers aside, she slipped down to pad barefoot across the stone floor to the window and push open the shutters.

Outside, the end of October and a fine, silvery haze burnished the high hills. The great peak of Ruadh-stac Mór at the upper end of the glen shone like a mountain in another, magical world. The slopes of Glen Grudidh glowed dimly with the faded purple and lavender of heather and the ghosts of bracken, red and yellow among the brown.

She took a deep breath, then snatched her shawl from its peg on the wall and raced down through the long house.

Tigh Grudidh—the name of the house in Gaelic, the language of the Scottish Highlands—was one room wide and one storey high, and stepped down a sloping field like four houses set end to end. Jamesina's father, Murdoch Mackenzie, had added the second "house" when he leased the land from the laird of Gairloch, and the last one when Jamesina was a baby, a month before he took up his sword and pistol and went to war.

Allan Graeme—Jamesina's uncle-by-marriage and the farm's manager while her father, now an outlaw, was in exile in France—stood with his broad back blocking the doorway from the dining parlor into the kitchen. Jamesina slipped up behind him to listen. She recognized the voice of Big Donald Mackenzie, one of the laird's manservants, or "gillies."

"Indeed," Big Donald was saying, "in Scardroy they searched Callum Macrae's house, then burnt it. This morning a message came secretly to Sir Alexander from Edinburgh. The king's soldiers are out after Mackenzie of Grudidh." He reached for the horn cup Old Jessie had filled from an earthenware jug.

"Father? He's coming home?" Jamesina's hands flew to cover her mouth and nose as if to hold in the excitement. *Four years.* It had been four years since her father's last secret visit.

Her aunt Mairi's eyes were on Big Donald. "But why should they suppose Murdo is in Scotland at all?" she asked, fluttering her hands like nervous birds. Mairi was Jamesina's dead mother's youngest sister, the prettiest and flightiest of four.

Big Donald pushed the cup across the table toward Jessie in hope of more. He grinned. "'Tis said there's a lass who's engaged to wed a talkative lieutenant whose father is a colonel. The news comes from her. It seems there was a report from King George's spies in France that Murdo was seen embarking from Calais on the ship *Fenix*. This week past, the *Fenix* was reported off the Mull of Kintyre."

"As close as that?" Allan was startled but, seeing

Jamesina's anxious look, he smiled. "Don't fret. Your father is safe enough. There are a hundred places the French can put him ashore with no one the wiser."

Jamesina came all the way into the room. "Was Rorie with him?" she demanded eagerly. She sorely missed her youngest older brother, Rorie, who had gone with their father when he returned to France after his last visit.

Big Donald shook his head. "The letter did not say."

Mairi's voice was plaintive. "But why does Sir Alexander say we are not to go to Edinburgh for the winter?" Mairi looked forward all summer to the pleasures of winter in town.

"It is for the best," Allan said. "It would not be wise to remind the king's officials in Edinburgh that the outlaw Mackenzie of Grudidh has lands and cattle enough that we can afford to take his household and silver and servants to town for the winter. They might turn up on the doorstep to claim every last silver spoon and candlestick. And all the Grudidh lands."

"They could not!" Jamesina protested. "The lands are Sir Alexander's. Father is only his tacksman." The whole of the parish belonged to Sir Alexander Mackenzie, chief of the Gairloch Mackenzies, and the "tacksmen" leased their large farms from him.

"*Surely* they could not," Mairi agreed. "It's true that Murdo fought the king's men twice, at Culloden and after, and plotted to make Bonnie Prince Charlie king, and failed. But Sir Alexander never did—nor most of the Gairloch Mackenzies!"

"Aye, lass, but for not taking back Murdo's lease and bestowing it elsewhere, they can say the laird approved of his treason."

Jamesina's eyes blazed. "Treason! It is no treason to fight for a true king. It was war."

"So we may say," was Allan's mild answer. "As long as we say it only among friends."

Aunt Mairi brightened. "But three of Jamesina's brothers are in the English king's army now. Surely that makes up for their father's foolhardiness."

Her husband gave a snort of laughter, but looked at her fondly. With her fair hair still tousled from the pillow, and a plaid wrapped around her nightgown for decency, Mairi was as pretty as the princess of Isle Maree in the old tale.

"No, lass, that bird won't fly. The king and his generals know the Highland lads do not join the army for love of King George. There's no work for them here, and little game to be got when guns are forbidden. The law says they cannot even wear the kilt or plaid. They join up so that they may earn pay, carry muskets, and be in a good fight now and then. *And* wear kilts instead of the cursed, baggy, chafing breeches lowlanders wear."

"But you wear the kilt, Uncle," Jamesina objected.

Aunt Mairi, suddenly anxious, looked at him accusingly. "Yes, Allan, you do."

Allan Graeme nodded. "Aye, I do. But if a cry 'Redcoats coming from Kinlochewe!' goes up, I promise you I will come running home, and welcome them to Grudidh dressed in good, safe, gray breeches."

Jamesina caught Old Jessie's eye and giggled. Old Niall Mackenzie had vowed he would never give up wearing the kilt, as his father and grandfathers had done before him, not for all the kings since Solomon. One day an army patrol came along Loch Maree from Talladale while he was fishing in the loch. Old Niall undid his belt, folded up the length of plaid that made his kilt, tucked it under his shirt, and raced all the way home with his bare bottom peeping out from under his shirttail.

Mairi, Allan, and Big Donald saw what they were thinking, and had to laugh, too.

Aunt Mairi's smile faded first. "What must we do?"

"Nothing in haste," Allan said. "Jamesina is to ride this morning to your father's to join her cousins in the Halloweven celebrations. She still must."

Jamesina had forgotten. Hallowe'en, and she had forgotten!

"Dress quickly, Jamesina," her uncle said. "You will ride as far as Flowerdale with Big Donald, and then straight on to Amgaldale."

As she vanished, Allan Graeme said to his wife, "I must go tomorrow to speak with the laird and decide what is wisest to do."

"Does Sir Alexander stay or go this winter?" Mairi watched Big Donald with a last, faint gleam of hope.

"He is staying here, Mairi."

Mairi sighed. "I'm sorry for the loss of our winter in town. Jamesina will miss the outings, and paying calls on all our relations."

Allan gave Mairi a quizzical look, for Jamesina did not care a pin for paying visits, embroidering handkerchiefs, and listening to great-aunts gossiping over teacups.

Mairi blushed and added hastily, "But I am sorrier still that she must worry now for Murdo. If he truly is in Scotland. I—"

She stopped suddenly as Jamie reentered the room.

"Jamesina Mackenzie! Look what you are wearing—*trews!* No, Allan—and you, Donald, never you laugh. It isn't respectable. You dare not ride to Gairloch in trousers, Jamesina. I cannot allow it. Your aunt Murdina would think I had lost my wits."

Jamesina edged toward the door, past the servants'

box beds in the corner of the room. She looked down at the tight trousers—her brother Rorie's. "They're much safer to ride in than skirts," she protested. "And these are not tartan."

"Trews!" Mairi wailed as her niece darted out the door. "Oh, Allan, stop her. She *will* not learn to be a lady—and she has not had a bite to eat."

2

JAMESINA CLAPPED HER BROTHER RORIE'S OLD BLUE bonnet on her dark curls, thrust the toe of her shoe in the stirrup, and swung herself up into her little roan horse's saddle. The saddle was Rorie's, too. Jamesina hated riding sidesaddle, lady-fashion. It was good, too, to have grown tall enough at long last to mount without climbing upon a stone or asking a gillie's help.

Asked or no, suddenly there was Dougal, Old Hector Macrae's grandson, at her stirrup.

"Why are you here?" Jamesina demanded. "Is the Grudidh bonfire built already?"

"The others can see to the bonfire here," Dougal answered mildly. "I go with you to Amgaldale."

Jamesina's chin lifted haughtily. "I'm no infant, to need a nursemaid. *Two* nursemaids, since I ride with Big Donald Mackenzie. Go gather kale stalks for the fire, or help your grandfather mend the winter pasture wall. Whatever you like."

"I will go with you."

"I told you," Jamesina flared. "You will not."

An answer gleamed in Dougal's eyes, but he said nothing. With the twitch of a rein and a nudge from her heel, Jamesina moved her horse down to stand beside Big Donald's.

Allan Graeme came out of the house with Big Donald. "Tell the Old Laird I'll come to Flowerdale," he said.

"Aye, I—" Big Donald broke off suddenly. *"Hi, lass!"*

An impatient Jamesina had drummed her heels against the roan's sides and cantered off. In a moment she was riding at full gallop down the track toward the River Grudidh. Big Donald mounted and hurried after. Once across the river, among the rowan and oak trees, with their scattering of scarlet leaves and bright brown, he caught up with her and snatched hold of the roan's bridle. He slowed her to a trot, and then to a walk.

"What do you think you're at," he demanded angrily, "to put her cold to the gallop, and downhill? And running through water so fast, the beast can't see her footing among the stones? You might have broken her legs and your own head. Your head's your own, but 'tis a pity to kill a bonny mare."

Jamesina's cheeks reddened, but she lifted her head proudly. "You are right. I was impatient. I did not think. It was wrong."

Big Donald looked across at her as they rode out of the trees and along the track above the shore of Loch Maree. In her jacket, blue bonnet, and trews, with her chin in the air and hair tied back with a string of soft leather, she might have been one of her own cocky brothers. Jamesina's cheeks were still red as they jogged along, but from pleasure. Big Donald was very good-looking, and did not try to entertain her as if she were a child. He kept his eyes on the muddy rim of the track, the shadows among the trees, the yellow trout that rose to make a ripple on the surface of the loch as it snatched at a fly. Her father treated her just so.

It was along the small bay where tiny Grudidh Island stood offshore that the boy Dougal caught up with them. Jamesina scowled down at him as he trotted barefoot beside her.

"Dougal Macrae, why are you here? I already have a shadow."

"Aye," Dougal said. He was not even breathless. "But if one is good, two are better."

In the next two silent miles the lakeshore wavered away from their path, and then near again. Only when they came within sight of the great cluster of islands in the lake did Dougal give Jamesina a sly look and speak again, mocking her with fine words.

"Alas, you punish me with silence, my lady, but I've no choice. My aged grandfather, Hector Macrae, swore to Murdo, your father, that you would never in this world come to harm. Alas, Grandfather is old. He has a boil on his foot, and the days when he could run to keep up with a horse are past, so here am I."

Jamesina found it hard to be angry, or even to keep a straight face. She was glad, after all, to have Dougal come, and a little ashamed that she had spoken sharply. She and Dougal had been playmates when they were small, and companions since. But she said nothing. It was Big Donald who broke the silence. "Look there, in the water," he said, and pointed to two overlapping Vs of ripples, the wakes of two swimming roe deer, a stag and a doe.

Jamesina raised up in her stirrups. "They're swimming out to Eilian Southainn. Oh, how I wish I were riding him!"

"No, you don't." Big Donald laughed over his shoulder. "He'd shrug you off in the sky-gray water, she'd give you a knock on the head, and you and the lad would the both of you drown, for he would have to jump in after you."

"No, for he cannot swim," objected Jamesina, who could.

"Which is why he would drown," Donald agreed.

Jamesina watched the islands over her shoulder as they rode on. Her father often had promised to take her to Eilian Southainn, but then he had to flee the king's men and sail to France instead.

Past Talladale Farm and the Talladale woods, they crossed Garavaig Burn, the stream below the falls, and moved into Slattadale Forest in silence. Above Slattadale Farm, they climbed away from Loch Maree and over the hills toward Gairloch. Below, across the ford where the River Cearridh bent toward the loch, the right-hand path led to Amgaldale, Jamesina's grandfather's farm. Jamesina thumped the mare's sides and splashed across, with Dougal still at her stirrup. Big Donald sat on the laird's black horse and watched them go.

On the other side, Jamesina turned to call back, "Thank you for your company." After a moment she called again. "Shouldn't you be off to Flowerdale? I know the way to Amgaldale, and this Dougal is stuck to me fast as a goosegrass bur."

Big Donald only grinned and nodded up his own road, where an old woman carrying on her back a basket of seaweed for her garden limped toward him from Cathar Bheag.

"Good morning to you, Rebecca," he called as she came near. He slipped from the saddle. "Come, ride over the stream. I'll carry your kelp."

"Bless you, Donald, lad," the old woman exclaimed. As he lifted her into the saddle, she peered across the stream and gave a cackle of laughter. "Is it Grudidh's daughter I see across the water? In *trews?*"

Jamesina scowled and turned the roan, urging her along the Amgaldale track through the trees.

Dougal kept pace beside her. "You cannot blame old Becca for gawping," he said. "If I were to put on a petticoat and gown, you would gawp at me."

"Did I ask for your opinion, Dougal Macrae?" The thought of Dougal in a petticoat and gown was so comical—and unsettling—that Jamesina spoke more sharply than she meant to.

"No." He was unbothered. "'Tis free. You're welcome to it without asking."

"Now, why would I want it," she asked airily, "if it is worth nothing?" She urged the roan to a gallop, leaving her shadow behind. For the first time since Talladale she felt cheerful. It was not often that she won the last word with Dougal.

"*Gealtaire!* Coward!" he called after her. "The air is free, but you do not stop breathing it, I see."

3

SUMMONED BY A WIDE-EYED SERVANT GIRL, AUNT Murdina came hurrying to the door. Floury hands on her hips, she watched in silence as Jamesina dismounted and handed the reins to one of the gillies. Her aunt's shocked stare was so fierce that—even though Jamesina felt that everyone was making a great fuss over nothing—her feet began to drag. To her surprise, Aunt Murdina vanished with a swirl of her skirts. Jamesina's grandfather appeared on the doorstep in her place.

"Who's this?" Roderick Mackenzie exclaimed. "A strange lad come from Grudidh with young Dougal?" He held out his arms to fold her in a warm hug that smelled of peat smoke, damp wool, hard and sweaty work, and whisky. "A strange lad, indeed. Come dressed to help bring the cattle down, have you?"

"Nonsense!" Murdina reappeared with a broad plaid spread out to fold around her niece. "You imp," she scolded. "Wrap yourself up before anyone else sees you. You're almost thirteen. Too old for such mischief. Go along up to your cousins' room, where you'll find a blue gown hanging behind the door. It should fit. 'Tis your good fortune that Johanna's grown out of it, and Isobel's not yet grown in."

"Yes, Aunt," Jamesina said meekly.

"Then," her aunt went on, "since Isobel is watching your aunt Mali's wee baby, and Mali and Esther and Fiona are helping me with the baking, when you've changed you may take the little ones off to cut bracken for the bonfire."

"'Nonsense' yourself, Daughter." Big Rorie's voice was a cheerful rumble. "The children have laid their bonfire luck-stones. One for Jamie, too. The fire is half-built, and the young ones can fetch bracken without her. After she's had a bite to eat, my Jamie can ride up to the shielings. She's old enough now to be of use there. Your blue gown can wait until the cattle are down in their winter pastures, lass, for I want them all down before dark. I want none left to be brought down tomorrow."

"But, Father—" Murdina began.

"Tcha! I don't care a bean for the trews. It isn't," he added in solemn mischief, "as if the child meant to go louping over the turf and heather in no more than a kilt and bare bottom."

"Father!" Murdina drew herself up even straighter and stiffer than before. "For shame!"

Big Rorie frowned at his eldest daughter. "Murdina, if you can show me where in the Scriptures the Good Lord forbids a touch of merriment, then I'll out-gloom the minister. If you cannot, then hold your tongue."

Murdina shook her head. "Very well. I leave Jamesina to you."

With a nod, she swept back into the house to her baking, and Jamesina smiled after her.

Rorie Mackenzie, seeing the triumph in her smile,

caught her gaze with his own, and spoke sternly. “Don’t ever look so, child. If her heart is shut up in a narrow box, ’tis because it has taken a great many hard knocks. But it still beats, and it loves you.”

“I know,” Jamesina said. She looked away, ashamed, but angry at the tears that threatened to show it.

“Then off with you to the kitchen for some bread and milk before we put you to work.”

By dusk that afternoon the last of the cattle and the few sheep and horses that had roamed the high hillsides and high moor all summer had been driven down and herded into the lower, winter pastures. If the work took an hour or two longer than it need have, games and chases and laughter had kept the younger workers cheerful. At the gates in the pastures’ stone and turf walls, Big Rorie and his oldest son, Jamesina’s uncle Angus, separated the young animals from their mothers for the first time, and gave them their new names. The calves now were to be called stirks, the lambs sheep, and the foals colts and fillies.

With the stock safely shut in their fresh fields for the winter, the young people made their way toward the dark, waiting bonfire, and sang as they went. The only gloom at Amgaldale was indoors in the big farmhouse. The fire on the kitchen hearth and all of the candles had been put out, as they were on every All Hallows’ Eve. Murdina was muttering darkly as she and her sister Mali filled a basket with bannocks. They had baked enough for their own children and the cousins and tenant families from the ten crowded small houses of the clachan on the near hillside.

“Hallowe’en!” Murdina grumbled. “Next, our father will have us roasting sheep’s heads for Saint Andrew’s

Day, and after, when the little ones go out to look for wild carrots and happen to find a forked root, he'll teach them the old charm to say when they rub it. Sinful foolishness! Oh, and *then* we will celebrate Christmas, too, though the ministers of the church forbid it."

"Yes, sister," Mali said mildly as Jamesina, in Johanna's blue gown, and her cousin Neil appeared as dark shadows in the doorway.

"Grandfather says it is time for the coal," Jamesina announced.

"Here, then." Murdina felt for the small bowl on the table. She took from it the leaf-wrapped parcel that held the last coal from the hearth fire in a nest of peat moss wound around with grass. It was the same each year. The fires in every house on the farm were doused, to be relit the next day from the "need-fire" that was lit from Amgaldale's last coal. Even Murdina's heart stirred at the knowledge that the fire cupped in her hand had first been lit a hundred years or two or three ago. No one knew how many. She handed it to young Neil and followed the children and Mali with her baby up past the huddled houses of the clachan.

At the edge of the dark bonfire, a twig with a bit of lint twisted around it was lit from the coal Neil carried, and a torch was lit from the twig. As the torch was handed to Davie, Jamesina's oldest cousin, Conal Macrae, Big Rorie's piper, filled the bag of his pipes with air and sent the melody of an old Mackenzie pibroch skirling out over the winter pastures. Davie held the torch high as he circled the pastures and returned to his starting place, and there he thrust the torch into the waiting bonfire.

Flame flared up through the bundles of dry bracken

with a crackle and roar. Fiercer ones still burst out from a tangle of broken poles and the staves of old tar barrels the children had begged from Jock Urquhart, the boat-maker in Gairloch. The young people cheered at the sight.

Next, Big Rorie and his son Duncan went into the pastures. Jamesina's grandfather bore a torch, and her uncle a pail of water mixed with salt and ammonia. Together they blessed each beast with the torchlight and a sprinkle from the pail, and Big Rorie chanted the age-old Gaelic rhyme, half charm and half prayer:

"Guiream tan a steach,
Air bhearn nan speach . . ."

"I drive the cattle within the gateway of the herds," it began, and wound on at last to *" . . . till bright daylight comes tomorrow . . . The Father, the Son, the Holy Spirit save you, and protect you, and tend you, till I or mine shall come to you again."*

Then everyone returned to the bonfire. Conal set to piping, the fiddler to fiddling, and the dancing began. Cousins and tenants were paired together, masters and servants, young and old. As the best dancers came to the center of the circle, the others kept time and shouted encouragement. The younger boys went out to race around the farm and the clachan and back, doing every mischief they could think of. They climbed onto thatch roofs to throw cabbages down the chimneys or to block the smoke holes with turf. They wedged doors fast with bits of wood at the bottom, and they carried away the gate to Big Rorie's kitchen garden.

The young men, while they were not dancing, ate and drank and carried on building a cairn of stones.

Some time long after midnight, when the bonfire had burnt down to embers and no more fuel was to be had, the coals would be heaped on top of the cairn. Several of the young men would stay to guard and feed this "need-fire" until morning. At dawn every household on the Amgaldale farm would bring a handful of moss and wrap up a bit of the need-fire in it to light their own fires anew for the year to come.

While the older folk—even Murdina—danced the old reels of their childhood, the bigger girls climbed as far above the bonfire as its light would reach. There they tried all the magic spells they knew to learn their futures. The number of grains on an oat stalk could tell how many children a girl could be given. Nine clumps of grass dug out and laid in a row, when counted nine times, were supposed to make a sweetheart appear.

"Look!" said Jamesina's cousin Margaret, who was eighteen and soon to marry a young man from Kinlochewe. Margaret reached into a pocket of her gown and brought out an apple and a small silver knife. From the gown's other pocket she drew a small mirror in a round silver frame. She gave the apple and knife to Johanna.

"Cut it into three," she prompted. "And each third again into three. Good. Now, you must eat eight of the pieces."

The girls watched expectantly as Johanna ate.

Margaret nodded. "Now put the ninth piece on the tip of the knife. You must hold the knife and apple over your left shoulder—yes—and the mirror over your right. No, like this—until you can see the bit of apple in it. Can you? Then you must hold it there and watch it until the spell makes your sweetheart come to eat it."

Solemnly, but on the edge of giggles, the girls

watched as Johanna peered earnestly into the little mirror and tried hard to keep the slice of apple in sight.

"Oh!" they all cried as the apple slipped from the knife tip.

"Let me try again!" Johanna scrambled to her feet. "I'll go down for more apples." And she lifted up her skirts and plunged away down the hill.

One of the girls nudged Jamesina. "Johanna wants to see your Dougal Macrae in the mirror."

Jamesina did not seem to hear. In the midst of her cousins she felt shadows press close around her, and it seemed that if she were to reach out a hand the girls would not be there. That her hand might pass through them. . . .

Margaret leaned toward her. "And whom would you wish to see, Cousin?" she teased. "I have one more apple in my pocket."

Jamesina blinked. "I? No one," she said slowly. "They all like themselves much too much."

"Even better!" Margaret held out the apple. "For wishing does not help. You—*Jamesina?*"

The girls' voices seemed very far away to Jamesina. Then the darkness swallowed them up, and vanished.

She stood on a bare slope in a fine mist, and watched two small figures toil up along the side of a rocky burn that flowed down a fold between two knees of the hill. Other figures, red-coated, crept through the heather far below them. Soldiers. Not hurrying. Watchful. Like a shooting party waiting for their dogs to flush out the game. And then the mist wiped them all away. In the same moment, a shadowy movement caught at the corner of her eye, and she turned. Not far off above her on the slope, three kilted shadows stood in the mist. In the mist, the red of their coats was faded, bloodless. As she watched, one lifted an arm to point downward. Her heart stopped at the sight. Though their eyes were shadowed and their faces drawn, she knew them all. Tall Kenneth of the gentle smile. Broad-shouldered Davie. Brave Donald. Her brothers.

In panic, Jamesina closed her eyes, but even with them closed she saw the climbers below lift up their heads. When she saw the two faces that stared upward, she knew them, too.

Her father and her youngest brother, Rorie.

Jamesina screamed.

4

Mairi and Allan Graeme rode into Amgaldale in the hour after first light. In the farmhouse several of the younger children who had fallen asleep and been carried home early were awake again, and Mali was keeping them quiet with the old tale of Whuppity Stoorie. The story broke off when she saw the Graemes.

"Oh, Mairi! I am so glad you are here." Mali rose and threw her arms around her younger sister. "Jamesina has had either a brainstorm or a sad fright," she said. "Murdina told the girls to hold their tongues, but I am sure that by now everyone knows of it. She's up in the girls' room."

Mairi and Allan climbed the narrow stone stair. In Johanna and Isobel's shadowy room, Murdina sat on a chair beside the bed, asleep, leaning forward with her arms around Jamesina. Jamesina lay curled on her side. Her face was pale in the shadows, and tear-streaked, and her hands were clasped under her cheek. Dougal Macrae sat on the floor beside them, fast asleep with his head pillowed on his arms crossed on his knees. Johanna and Isobel and their cousin Margaret were curled up together, still wide-eyed, and whispering. They sat up when they saw their aunt and uncle, and ten-year-old Isobel scrambled to the edge of the bed. "It was the *dà shealladh,*" she said excitedly. "The second sight. She was seeing spirits!"

"Hush!" Johanna hissed. She gave her little sister a shove. "You'll waken Mother."

Everyone glanced at Murdina, who looked painfully uncomfortable. She had slumped sideways almost off her chair onto the bed, one hand lying limp on Jamesina's dark red curls, as if she had been stroking them.

"Tell us," Mairi whispered. "Quietly."

"We—all but the little girls"—Johanna frowned at Isobel—"were trying to divine who would be our sweethearts."

"Working magic?" Allan Graeme's eyebrows lifted in surprise, then lowered in a frown.

Mairi sat on the edge of the girls' bed. "Girls always do on Hallowe'en. Go on, Johanna."

Johanna nodded toward the oldest of the three. "It was Cousin Margaret's mirror, you see. We were cutting apples into nines and trying to see our husbands over our shoulders." She looked at her aunt doubtfully, as if it were unlikely that anyone so pretty as Mairi had ever needed a mirror to tell her whether this boy or that liked her. But Mairi only nodded, and waited.

"Then we told Jamesina to try, but as soon as she lifted the mirror she dropped it. It was dark, and we were feeling through the grass for it when she made a—a queer strangled sort of sound."

"Like a shout that wants to get out but can't," Isobel put in eagerly. Her eyes were round as an owl's with excitement, and she shivered happily. "She stood up, straight and stiff as a post, and her arms out straight, like this—"

Isobel stood up on her knees on the bed and held her arms out straight before her, with her hands up and fingers spread as if to ward off a danger.

"She wasn't making horrid faces like that," Johanna snapped. She pulled her sister down again.

Margaret had been silent. Alone of the three, she appeared more anxious than excited. "Jamesina said, 'No,'" she said. "Not aloud. Just her lips. Three times, 'No, no, no!' Then she fell down in a faint. Afterward she couldn't say what happened. Aunt Murdina says it was my fault—but it wasn't anything to do with the mirror. Really, it wasn't."

"I *told* you," Isobel insisted loudly. "It was the Second Sight. She was seeing *taibhsean*."

Across the room, Murdina stirred and raised herself stiffly. *"Taibhsean?"* She placed a careful hand over Jamesina's ear.

"If there are such things as visions of dead souls or living," she whispered fiercely, "they come from the Devil, and must be prayed away."

"Yes, Aunt," Margaret said, and bowed her head as if she meant to begin that instant.

"Seadh a' Mhathair," said both of Murdina's daughters. "Yes, Mother." But they said it as though they would have argued if they dared.

Mairi rose, even more worried than at first. "Jamesina? Oh, sister, she is so white. She is always too brown from being out in all weathers, but now she is pale as skimmed milk. Why doesn't she wake?"

Murdina reached out to give Jamesina a shake. "Wake up, lass," she said briskly. "The day waits for us to be up and doing."

Jamesina opened her eyes, but for a moment did not

move. Then she pushed herself up and sat rubbing her eyes. Mairi held out her arms and crossed the room in two steps.

"O, Piuthar-Màthar," Jamesina wailed, and she sprang up from the bed to meet Mairi's embrace.

Behind them, Murdina sat silent for a moment, watching, then rose and moved to the shuttered window. She stretched and rubbed at her side again, then opened the shutters and leaned out into the gray morning.

"Ho! There go Christy and Janet to fetch their need-fire, and here are we with a houseful of hungry and thirsty kinsmen, and no cookfire yet for the kettles. Isobel! Run down to the cupboard to find the little pot with the lid. Take a bit of peat to put in it, and go out to the cairn to fetch us a good coal. Go! Run, child! And Margaret and Janet—I hear Old William downstairs still sawing on his violin, and Toothless Ian singing away like a rusty hinge. Sweep them out and off to their own beds with a broom if you must, and wake Sarah the cook if she's not already stirring. We have fifteen to feed for breakfast."

Shooing the girls before her, she went out and closed the door behind her.

Mairi drew Jamesina back to the bed and sat down beside her to brush a few damp, untidy tendrils of hair back from her forehead. Allan Graeme smiled down at them.

"There, you'll be fine, now," he said. "It was only the dark, and the spells, and the firelight—and its being Hallowe'en—that frightened you."

"No." Jamesina's face stayed buried in her aunt's shoulder. "No. I didn't want to see, but I couldn't look away. Oh, Aunt Mairi, take me home to Grudidh."

Allan hesitated for a moment, then asked, "What was it that you didn't want to see, Jamesina?"

"Leave the child alone," Mairi protested quickly. "'Tis best forgotten."

"No." Jamesina pulled free and lifted dark, shadowed eyes to watch her uncle as she told what she had seen.

"Well, there you are," Allan Graeme said, as heartily as he could manage. "It is all a nonsense. Your brothers are in Canada, fighting Frenchmen and Indians, not on a Scottish hillside. Your father is alive and well, whether in Scotland or in France."

Mairi clenched her hands together in her lap so tightly that her knuckles whitened. "But—but what if young Isobel is right? That it was the Second Sight. *Tannasg* and *Tamhasg*, the ghosts of the dead and of the living, *can* show themselves."

"Aye," said Allan, to soothe her, though he did not believe in such things. "Though it is men who are the seers."

"But sometimes a woman or child," Mairi answered fearfully.

"They're not dead!" Jamesina said desperately. "I saw them, but they can't be!"

A soft tap came at the door. Margaret looked in, with Isobel at her elbow.

"Sir Alexander has sent for Grandfather," Margaret said. "At least, I suppose there was a messenger, but no one saw him. Grandfather is gone already, and says that you should follow at once, Uncle."

"And," Isobel offered in a wide-eyed rush, "Johanna says when the bonfire ashes were swept away, Jamesina's stone was *gone*. Johanna says it means—"

She was cut off in mid-flow as Margaret pulled her back into the next room and closed the door after them.

Jamesina looked at her uncle in sudden panic. "Why does Sir Alexander wish to see Grandfather, and you?"

"It is nothing new, child. No reason to trouble yourself. I spoke with Sir Alexander yesterday about your father's coming. He said that he would have a word with Big Rorie this morning. And now he has heard that I am here, too. That is all, I promise you."

The morning mist had turned into a fine rain before Big Rorie Mackenzie rode up the lane to Flowerdale House. A groom, rumpled and yawning as if he, too, had been up all night, appeared to take the old man's horse. The front door was opened by Big Donald, who was bleary-eyed but as scrubbed and combed, as ironed and polished, as on a Sunday.

"Sir Alexander?" Donald blinked like a sleepy hawk. "He sent no one to Amgaldale to fetch you. He went to his bed only an hour ago. But come in, Big Rorie, out of the weather."

At that, it was old Rorie's turn to blink, though with his curly white hair and whiskers he looked more like a baffled winter owl. "Perhaps—I was sitting up by the new fire. Perhaps I dreamed it," he said uncertainly, turning at the sound of uneven footsteps on the graveled path.

The man who came stumbling toward the house wore loose woolen breeches and a muddy green coat. The bonnet he wore bore a sprig of holly. He stopped, breathless, beside Big Rorie.

"The laird's abed, did you say?" the man asked when he had caught his breath. "Then root him out, man! Mackenzie of Grudidh and his lad have been murdered by the redcoats."

5

THE PARLOR AT AMGALDALE WAS SO FULL OF ANGER THAT it seemed as if the air itself might explode, blowing the roof away and letting in the rain. Allan Graeme listened to Big Rorie in a daze of grief and fury. Murdo Mackenzie of Grudidh had been more to him than his employer and his wife's brother-in-law. If they had been brothers, he could not have been dearer. Murdina, Mali, and Mairi sat with Jamesina on the pine settle. Handsome though they were, they made young Dougal Macrae think of three fierce, black-faced ewes protecting their sister's lamb.

Jamesina, her tears dried for the present, sat with her head down and hands folded in her lap. She did not look up as her grandfather drew a deep breath and spoke. "It is Jamesina we must think of now. If the report is true, she and Grudidh are in danger."

Young Dougal Macrae's watchful gaze fixed on Big Rorie. *Danger?* he seemed to be thinking. *How?*

"The law of Scotland is clear," the old man explained.

"If by some sad fate my soldier grandsons in Canada truly *are* dead, all that was Murdo's will be hers, absolutely. That includes the lease of the Grudidh lands. But King George and the English law will disagree. They will try to say that Murdo was a traitor, and that from the day he was proclaimed a traitor, all that he owned became the property of the Crown."

Jamesina did not stir, not even at the hateful word "traitor." Their words meant nothing to her. The world had cracked apart. Before, apart or together, her father and brothers had made a circle that held her safe and happy at its center, and held around itself a world of circles: the families of the farm, the clan, the kingdom. . . . All broken.

Mali's husband, Callum Maclennan, paused in his pacing up and down. "But, Big Rorie—the land is Sir Alexander's. That at least is safe."

Big Rorie nodded. "Aye, it is his, but as Allan says, the English can claim that he should have canceled the lease when Murdo was outlawed. They may say that because he did not, he winked at treason. Worse, they might claim that he shared that treason, and use it as an excuse to take more from him than the Grudidh lands."

Allan Graeme nodded. "But as Mairi says, Kenneth, Davie, and Donald are serving the king in Montgomery's Highlanders. What better proof of Grudidh loyalty than that?"

"They are dead," Jamesina whispered. She raised her head a little, but only to lean and rest it on Mairi's shoulder.

"If they are," Big Rorie said sternly, "the king's officials may do more than claim the lease and title to the Grudidh lands. They may claim Jamesina, too."

"Never!" young Dougal cried. As he leaped to his

feet, he saw all eyes turn to him, and his cheeks burned with embarrassment. Still, he spoke out. "They would not dare. Not in Mackenzie country."

Jamesina herself was startled a little into life. "Take me?"

"Aye, as an orphan and ward of the Crown," her grandfather said grimly, "and cart you off to Edinburgh or the south, to be married off one day to some outlander to whom the king owes a small favor."

Jamesina stared blankly.

"Even if not," Big Rorie went on, "others closer at hand will turn a hungry eye this way. In Scotland there are landless younger sons aplenty, and greedy older ones, with sharp eyes for such a chance. They will not be forgetting that your father may have had a claim to Redcastle and its lands."

"I don't care," she whispered. "Not if they're all dead. And they are."

"Nonsense!" Murdina burst out. "You would soon be wishing yourself home if you found yourself wed to a Campbell or some other old enemy who held his kittle and cattle more dear to him than his wife. Or a Southern ninny in a velvet coat and satin breeches!"

Murdina grew more indignant with every word, until she fairly spat them out. Despite the gloom that filled the parlor, Big Rorie found himself half smiling at his oldest daughter's struggles to hide from herself the softness of her own heart.

Allan Graeme shifted impatiently on his chair. "Very well, then, Big Rorie—what is it we are to do?"

The older man sat back in his own chair and watched them all. "Just this: I proposed, and Sir Alexander agreed, that there is no Jamesina Mackenzie, no daughter of Mackenzie of Grudidh here, or in Glen Grudidh.

She may be with his kinsmen in Cromarty. She may be safe in France."

For a moment the room was silent, and only the puzzled frowns asked questions. Mairi, bewildered, clutching Jamesina's hand, was first to speak. "Father, you *must* not send her away!"

As the others echoed her, Big Rorie held up his hands for silence. "'Twas Jamesina who gave me the idea. Today young James Maclennan and his cousin Dougal have come to Amgaldale from Banff to be fostered by their uncle, Callum Maclennan, under the roof of Callum's wife's father. Come, Jamie, Dougal—stand and meet your kinsmen."

Dougal was baffled. Jamesina looked uncertainly from one face to another.

"*James?*" Allan Graeme laughed aloud—the first laughter the house had heard since sunrise. He sobered at once, but the warmth in his voice as he said, "It seems a good answer," was enough to make Mairi brighten in spite of her puzzlement. Dougal suddenly grinned, and Callum laughed, too.

"I pray for sons—" Callum shook his head. "And these two are my reward?"

Murdina drew a sharp breath, but kept her mouth tight shut. Jamesina still was mystified.

"The trews, lass!" Allan, her uncle, exclaimed. "The trews! You'll be James Maclennan and wearing trousers until you're heartily sick of them and the life that goes with them."

Big Rorie shook his head. "Not so long as that, I hope."

"Oh, Grandfather, I wish *I* could wear trews," cried Isobel before her mother could hush her.

Mairi looked doubtfully from her father to her husband. "But it won't be good for Jamesina. If she takes to galloping and striding around and playing shinty, she'll forget what it is to be a lady."

Big Rorie gave his youngest and prettiest daughter, his pet, a wry look. "Would you rather have her ladylike or safe? She must save the fine manners for a gentler time, my dear."

He became all business. "Sir Alexander will take back the lease of the Grudidh lands, Jamesina, but will keep your uncle Allan on as factor. When word is spread that you are poor as well as orphaned, you may safely put on your skirts again. And when Kenneth and Davie and Donald come home, Kenneth shall have the lease again, and all will be well."

Murdina gave a disapproving snort but, being Murdina and always practical, rose to say briskly, "Then Allan and Mairi must leave at once for Grudidh. If the soldiers were at Scardroy yesterday, they will not be long in coming to Loch Maree. And take an extra horse or two," she added. "Good, strong hampers, too. Jamesina's things must not be found at Grudidh. You must pack up the silver, Mairi. If there is time, the good china and goblets. They'll only be smashed if soldiers come rummaging through the house."

The soldiers did come. Finding nothing in Grudidh House worth the taking, they burned it. Afterward, Allan Graeme joked grimly that the house was stretched out so long that they had a hard time of it. The thatch burned in the end, but it was so damp from the rains that at first the flames would not take hold. The soldiers had to build a blaze in each room to light the thatch from below—and nearly smothered themselves in the smoke.

The soldiers killed a cow to roast over their cookfire,

and took the only horse left in the barn, but most of the cattle had been driven into the forest for safekeeping and penned there. The captain who commanded the troop, being an intelligent man who did not know how many clansmen the forest and the slopes above might be hiding, kept his men well in hand and marched them out four abreast the way they had come.

But it was only the first danger that had passed.

The report of the death of Murdo and Little Rorie Mackenzie proved true, but no news came from Canada. The letter sent to Kenneth Mackenzie, in care of Captain Hugh Mackenzie of Montgomery's Highlanders, would not reach the regiment in the Colonies for months.

Jamesina became James. Her grandfather had always called her Jamie, and so the name came easily to everyone's tongue.

And Murdina and Mairi's misgivings were proved right. Jamie took to her new freedom despite the grief that swept over her in unexpected tides and could turn the sunniest sky gray. The little world of Amgaldale grew wider, its sky higher. Big Rorie entered into the masquerade with a glee that made Murdina grumble. He sent to Dingwall for a tutor for "Callum Maclennan's foster sons." He sent off their measurements to a tailor in Edinburgh, for new outfits. It became easier each week for Jamesina to shut away her grief by shedding Jamesina.

When the tutor, a young man named Ian Maclaren, came, Dougal—who could barely read or write in Gaelic—found himself having to learn to read and write English, and to speak it properly. Jamie found his struggles entertaining until her own rusty Latin—her last lesson had been when she was nine—earned her as many extra hours of work as Dougal's English.

Beyond the big farmhouse, Jamie discovered a world where no one had to give her a hand over rough rocks so that she would have a hand free to hold up her skirts. No one splashed into the River Cearridh to help her when she slipped on a rock and dropped her fishing rod. When Dougal once did offer her a hand, she warned him off with a flare of temper.

"Take care you don't cut yourself on that sharp tongue," he answered mildly.

Dougal was a good companion. Jamie herself was, and was not. One morning she might be eager for a climb, full of wonder at the hawks that soared wide circles over Sidhean Mór, and shouting, "I want a hawk! I *must* have a hawk!" An hour later she might be shadowed by a terror that in that very hour the letter carrier was on his way from Dingwall, carrying the dreadful news from Canada. Dougal watched her soar and sink, and waited for the next day.

December came, and winter in earnest. Christmas came, and with it news from the far side of the sea that was worse than no news. The 77th Regiment of Highlanders, to which the three Mackenzie brothers belonged, had been sent to fight the French and Indians in the far west of the Pennsylvania Colony. In October they had captured Fort Duquesne, but only after an earlier defeat that cost the 77th many lives. The names of Jamie's brothers were not listed, but the vague mention of "other losses" haunted the farmhouse at Amgaldale.

The new year came in at Amgaldale with the music and dancing of a *ceilidh,* but not the usual high spirits. Once in January, despite the bitter weather, the red coats of an army patrol were spied on a hill above Kernsary. Even so, almost every hour she was not at work in the parlor-schoolroom, Jamie spent out-of-doors and away from her aunts' watchful concern and kindnesses.

On a rainy Monday in January she rode out with Dougal through Gairloch and Strath toward the Sand River, near where the loch met the sea. His mother's old grandmother lived there still, at ninety-two. They took with them Big Rorie's birthday gifts to her of a salmon from the smokehouse and a bottle of brandy.

The clachan where Dougal's great-grandmother lived with a grandson and his wife and children was a huddle of low houses, partly stone and mostly sod, on the hillside. From the clachan, the view south and west was of the loch, the small, nearby island of Longa, and the sea and the great Isle of Skye beyond. The children there, a girl of nine and a boy of six, ran out to hold the horses. Jamie's mare stepped on the girl Fiona's bare foot, but after one brief shriek, Fiona refused to let go the reins and happily stood in the drizzle and stroked the shaggy neck while Dougal and Jamie went indoors.

The old woman's watery eyes lit up at the sight of the bottle, and Dougal laughed.

"D'you like that French tipple, then, Great-grandmother?"

"Oh, no!" The old woman shook her head and patted the brown bottle as she set it carefully on the table. "I've never put tongue to it. 'Tis nasty stuff, I'm sure, for the ministers say so. But to them that do drink spirits, it's worth three hens and two loads of peat for me."

At the end of the visit, she pressed a fresh-baked loaf of oat and barley bread on the "dear lads."

"'Twill do for a midday meal on your way home, and Ellen will slice a bit of the salmon to go with it.

'Tis a monstrous great fish for only we six."

When they left the cottage the rain had stopped, and Jamie decided over Dougal's objections that they would eat their lunch down on the shore. She was in no hurry to be back at Amgaldale. "The French call it a *pique-nique,*" she said airily, and turned the roan away from the track and down toward the loch.

There they rode along the sand to a tiny cove sheltered by a weathered spine of rock that thrust out into the water. The tide was at low ebb, and the sand littered with seashells. They perched on low, smooth rocks near the water's edge and, in friendly silence, ate the salmon with torn-off chunks of the bread, which was too fresh to cut with Dougal's dirk.

The sea and wind sang together in their ears, so that they heard too late the warning cry from the hillside above, and saw too late Dougal's cousin Fiona come bounding down the hill, half limping, her arms waving, pointing . . .

As Jamie and Dougal stared upward and strained to hear, at their backs a longboat angled into shore, behind the rocks. Three men scrambled out and, climbing upon the rocks, leaped down and seized them.

A voice shouted from the boat. *"Take the boys! Forget the girl. She's lame."*

Then Dougal's dirk was out, and he slashed at the man who held him, bringing blood. "Jamie!" he shouted. "Run!"

He lunged at the man who held her, but the third man sprang at him and struck hard at his arm with a short, thick cudgel, so that the dirk spun away, into the sand. Dougal gasped, and staggered, but kept on. Stumbling, he reached out with his good hand to grasp by the hair the man who struggled to hold Jamie, and jerked his head back so sharply that the man dropped where he stood.

The third man raised his cudgel again and swung it sideways at Dougal's head. Dougal dropped to the sand and lay as still as the stones beside him. On the hill above, Fiona screamed for help that was too far off to hear.

Jamie, in her fear and fury, snatched up Dougal's dirk. Scarcely knowing what she did, she stood over him, blade ready, and watched the cudgel's threatening motions.

She had forgotten both the man Dougal wounded and the voice that had called, "Forget the girl." An arm wrapped around her. A large hand that smelled of salt water and pitch clapped over her mouth and eyes. A third hand gripped her wrist like iron, and the dirk dropped from her fingers.

She heard one—the fourth man?—say roughly, "You've kilt him, you fool. Leave'm lie." And then she dropped into darkness.

At Sea

1758

6

THE SOBS WERE QUIET, THE COUGHS MUFFLED, YET THEY filled the empty spaces in the darkness between the groan of wood against wood and the *lap-lap-lap* of water.

Jamie stirred in her sleep. The feather bed was strangely hard, and her hip ached. She reached out a hand to grope for the thick, soft blanket, but her fingers met only a thin, scratchy wool. Dark air, bitterly cold, pressed in on her, and it stank. Half awake, uneasy, she reached out from under the strange blanket to feel for the sheet and feather bed. Instead, her fingers touched rough wood—a wooden floor?

That floor rose beneath her. The *lap-lap-lap* of water . . .

In the darkness that swung and creaked and sighed around her, Jamie sat bolt upright, like a frightened hare sitting up tall to scan the fox-haunted heather. Breathless, eyes wide, seeing nothing, she rose and fell and shuddered with the floor as it juddered beneath her.

The sobs beside her were thin as a whisper. A child's,

she thought. She heard smothered coughs, too, some sharp as a dog's bark, others deep-wracked and breathless. It was all too real, the smell too foul, for a dream, yet . . .

A hand brushed her arm. It was a child's, bony, and rough, and cold. Mistrustfully, Jamie reached out, too, and found a wrist and arm that trembled with a bone-deep shiver. The sobs stopped. There was a sniffling like a small, miserable animal's, and two bony hands captured one of Jamie's. A small, bony body inched closer until a head nestled into her side and an arm crept across her middle.

Jamie held her breath and lay still under the child's arm. Strange that it should feel so solid, so real. A strange dream. Nothing happened in it. Only darkness and sleepers sleeping, nothing more. Dreams moved. They raced or ambled. They slipped from now into time past, or from a "here" into a "there" as swiftly as stepping through a door. Perhaps . . .

Jamie awoke hours later to a darkness mingled with gray shadow. Dim light came from somewhere above, not far off. Overhead she heard a thumping. A dim voice called out words that made no sense. *"Bowse upon the tack, there! Bowse away!"* Her eyelids were heavy, too heavy to hold open. She closed them quickly, unsure whether the tightness in her middle was nausea or hunger.

A high squeak suddenly shrilled in her ear. "Ye're no lad—you're a lass!"

Jamie opened her eyes to squint into the darkness. A small figure, a boy of seven or eight, knelt beside her, eyes wide in wonder. He was small for his size, and bony as a starveling goat. His once-white shirt, green waistcoat, and brown breeches were so darkened by grime and stained with food and grease that when he did not move, his grayness blurred into the shadows. Only the streaks of old tear tracks on his cheeks showed that gray was not their natural color.

Suddenly something smaller and gray streaked across her blanket. A rat!

Jamie bit back a shriek of fright, and sat up with a shudder. *The rocks and sand at Big Sand. She and Dougal eating. Fiona's cry, and the men . . .* In a rush, she remembered. *Dougal . . .*

She was on a ship. They had carried her onboard a ship.

"*'Tis* a lass!"

Another voice groaned out of the darkness, "Shut your gabble, Skrankie!"

"What does he mean, 'a lass'?" came a sleepy grumble nearby. Jamie peered around her in alarm. The dim light that fell through a heavy wooden grating some twenty feet away showed her that she was in a wide, low space, and surrounded by blanket-covered bodies. Many were astir, sitting up or stretching out arms. Some nearer at hand heard the whispers and rose to their hands and knees.

"What's afoot?" they murmured to their neighbors.

"What's all the cushle-mushle?"

"Skrankie says the new lad's a girl."

Soft snorts of laughter rippled away as the word spread, so that the blankets heaved like a rough, gray sea. A sea of boys that lapped up against the walls at either side of the deck. Forty or more lay before and behind her. "She *is,*" the boy Skrankie insisted, more quietly this time. "She smells like bread. And soap, and lavendy flowers, like my auntie," he said, and began to weep again.

"Ah, shut the shergar up," someone grumbled.

Most of the blankets lay still again, but one boy threw his off and raised up on his knees to stare at Jamie. "'Tis all clitter-clatter. He's no' sae fodgel as a lass."

Jamie frowned. "Clitter-clatter" seemed clear enough. It must mean something like "silly chatter"—but, "fodgel"? "Shergar"? They were Lowland Scots, and their heavily accented English, thick with unfamiliar words, made them hard for her to understand.

"De' is ciall 'dha, 'fodgel'?" she asked.

"Can ye no' speak the English? We dinna comprehend such Highland clytach," one said as a handful more sat up.

"Aye," she snapped. "*I* speak English. I asked what 'fodgel' means."

"Only that ye're a wee bit—stringy for a lass," one piped up.

With an effort, Jamie held her tongue. To be taken for a boy by a stranger—she felt a stirring of interest. But, surely, they would find her out. Surely . . .

A thin, gangly boy of about fifteen with lank, dark hair rose, wrapped his blanket around his shoulders, and threaded his way toward Jamie for a closer look. From the way the others watched him—curious, expectant—he appeared to be, if not their leader, at least someone they judged worth listening to.

"Where am I?" Jamie asked quickly. "What ship is this, and why am I here?"

"'Tis the *Sparrowhawk,* bound for Glasgow." He ignored her last question. "I am Archie Gordon, of Aberdeen. They call me Attercap. But who are you? What waters did they fish you from?"

"From Loch Gairloch. I am Jamie Mackenzie, of Amgaldale," she answered boldly as she rose. She hoped they could not hear in her voice that she was still shaking from the strangeness of it all. "Men attacked us on the sands at Big Sand. We saw no ship. It must have stood off behind Longa Island. My—my foster brother, Dougal. They killed Dougal." Her stomach heaved at the memory of Dougal lying on the sand, and she had to force herself to swallow. "Who are they? Why did they attack us? Why are you all here?"

Attercap gave her a small quirk of a smile, and then grew grim. "Captain Lumsden and his men are 'spiriters.' They spirited you away. Stole you as they stole us." His voice was flat. "Four of us are dead. We sailed north around Scotland through great storms, and three fell ill and died of the cold. The fourth was a wee, homesick lad who wouldna eat. The seamen stitched them up in sailcloth and tipped them into the sea. Likely they saw you and decided to make up a part o' the loss."

"*Stolen?*" Jamie's cry came out as a whisper. Stolen? Not taken by her father's enemies?

"Aye. Snared like rabbits," said a bitter-faced boy with ears like jug handles, and a still-red scar upon his dirty cheek.

"But"—Jamie shook her head as if to clear it—"And they sail to Glasgow? It makes no sense. The Glasgow magistrates and their bailiffs will hear of it and stop them. It makes no sense."

Attercap shook his head. "Ye've taken hold of the cow horned end hindermost. 'Tis rich Glasgow merchants—likely magistrates themselves—have bought the *Sparrowhawk* from the old owners in Aberdeen. From Glasgow it sails to the Virginia Colony."

"*Virginia?* In America?"

"Aye, America. The far side of the sea." Attercap shivered under his blanket cloak.

Jamie's knees grew weak under her, and she sat down heavily on the deck. She rested her head upon her knees. *America.* Kenneth and Davie and Donald had gone to Canada and America, and were dead. Dead before her father, even, and dear Rorie. America.

A slow, thick voice spoke loudly into the silence. "Crookie says they mean to sell us for slaves, t' dig in the earth and live in holes, like beasties."

"Shut thy mouth, ye great lubbard," a voice shrilled. Jamie heard the sound of a scuffle and blow somewhere among the boys who crowded around her. The loud blubbing that followed the blow sounded eerily like the heartbroken tears of wee Niall, her aunt Mali's next-to-youngest, after an unexpected smack.

The blubberer was a big, moonfaced boy whose dirty fair hair hung over his eyes and ears. His attacker turned out to be Skrankie. Frail and pale the child might be, but he had the blank, baleful, stubborn stare of a goat.

"Hush, shush, ye great gowkie," Attercap told the big, round-faced boy impatiently. "Thy hubble-bubble will bring Mr. Marr doon on us. And ye, Skrankie, for why'd ye ding the poor fool? We all heard Crookie say the same."

"But 'tis a lie," the one called Skrankie quavered. "After Glasgow, we'll be on the way home to our mithers and aunties. Ye'll see!" After a moment he whined, "Any road, I hit him only a wee chap to the middle."

"Crookie is the cook's boy," Attercap explained to Jamie. "Have a care what ye say to him. He's like a squirrel who stores up nuts. He stores up all he hears and can cast it up word for word to the captain to make trouble. He—"

Attercap stopped abruptly as the heavy wooden grate covering the overhead hatch was raised, and a dark head and shoulders loomed above them against a gray sky. Jamie could make out only a dark, bearded face under a three-cornered hat.

"You, down there! Any more roarie argle-bargaining, and Cap'n Lumsden says he'll send Jemmy Dunn below wi' a belaying pin to ding some heads. You hear that?"

"Yes sir, Mr. Marr," Attercap answered quickly. He pushed his way through the knot of boys around Jamie, to stand next to the ladder in the patch of light beneath the hatch. "'Twas only a wee curfuffle. We'll no' put Mr. Dunn to the bother o' cracking our heads."

"So ye say," the first mate growled. "Back off the ladder, then. Here's Crookie and Cook and thy parritch." He straightened and vanished from view.

A redheaded, freckled boy in a canvas apron, and a red-nosed, red-cheeked man with a grin full of blackened, rotten teeth appeared in the hatch's frame. Between them, they hoisted a large kettle onto its rim and lowered it by rope onto the cover of the hatch that led to the ship's cargo hold below the boys' deck.

Two boys moved forward at Attercap's nod, but stepped back quickly as Mr. Marr reappeared.

"Is the new lad up and alive yet? Shove him over here, then, and be sharp about it." He moved away.

Jamie found herself lifted up and bundled through the press of boys ringing the hatch's patch of daylight. "'Tis likely the captain coming," one whispered as she passed. "Doff thy bonnet," another warned with a jab to her ribs. She found herself, bonnet in hand, standing beside the kettle of oatmeal and squinting up at a black shadow against the dull sky's brightness. The silhouette seemed huge.

"What's your name, lad?" it growled.

"Jamie Mackenzie of Amgaldale," she answered, still

squinting. Suddenly unbearably angry, she stood as tall as she could and added coldly, "And what may yours be, sir?"

The silence above and below was frightening. Beneath her breastbone, her stomach began to quiver from hunger and the nearness of the steaming oatmeal, but her squint held steady. She was thankful that, with the light at his back, she could not see the captain's eyes. Her knees might have quivered, too.

The shadow's heavy voice was low, but cold and hard. "'Tis Lumsden. Captain Lumsden. And isn't it the fine-spoken wee gentleman we've snared this time!"

"Sir, I demand—"

"'*Sir, you demand*'?" The captain raised his deep voice only a notch, but it cut through Jamie's like a steel blade through a willow wand. "Go softly, laddie. I advise ye to swallow the word 'demand' and not to cough it up again. Ye'll have no use for it these next eight or nine years. Raise thy voice to me again, and I'll have Mr. Marr haul ye up and beat a tattoo on thy backside ye'll not soon forget. Now, away with ye."

He vanished from the hatchway, but could be heard ordering the cook and his boy back to their galley, and shouting to a seaman to lock down the hatch grate.

Jamie stood frozen. She had never in her life been spoken to as if—as if she were muck beneath a stranger's boot. But fear thrust down the anger that rose in her throat. Fear had a new and bitter taste, a taste of iron, and her pride did not like it. She had faced anger before, had exchanged angry words, but they were always words taken back or softened when the anger cooled. The captain's cold contempt was not anger, but the sound of power. It said, "*You are nothing.*" Desperately, Jamie repeated to herself the last words her father spoke to her.

"You are Mackenzie of Grudidh while we are away, lass, and as good as any who walk the hills on two feet. Never you forget that. Or me."

"Never," she whispered fiercely now.

7

NEVER IS A LONG TIME.

The betweendecks space—the steerage in which the boys were shut up—was a dank, cold, low-ceilinged cargo hold. The rough planks of the hull wall were gray-black with coal dust from the *Sparrowhawk*'s early life as a collier. The decking underfoot, despite its tracked-in grime, showed here and there that it was new, and the *Sparrowhawk* recently refitted. Forward, toward the ship's bow, a second grated hatch let in cold air and a little more gray light. It was at the ship's stern, furthest from any curious ears listening at hatch gratings, that the boys crowded around to hear Jamie's story, to lick their shallow tin plates clean, to clutch their blankets close against the cold, and to tell their own tales.

Archie Gordon—Attercap—took back each finished plate and stowed it in a bag of netted rope. "They drag it through the sea to wash 'em," he explained as he looked at Jamie's plate and then handed it back. "Ye've a good lick or two there yet. Clean it proper. 'Tis a long day till dinner."

"Did they kill that Dougal, then?" another boy asked her.

"Aye, they did." Jamie did not lift her eyes from the battered plate. *It was my fault. My fault,* she thought. The porridge lay heavy as a great stone under her ribs.

Skrankie reached out to touch the side of her head. "They gived ye a lump like a gull's egg," he said as she winced away. "If my auntie were here, she'd souse it wi' vinegar."

"I'm near scomfished wi' thy blessed auntie," growled a boy with a dark bruise under one eye. "Keep the old hen in her cavvy, ye babby."

The boys' tales did not come easily. The older they were, the angrier and more shamed they felt for not seeing as lies the kind words that had caught them.

"Like wee birds that step into snares and end up in pies," one said bitterly.

"The last miles, they drove us like cattle," another said. "With clubs and whips and harsh words. And at Dyce, there was five, six women and men come running out of their kitchies and cow byres, all crying 'Spiriters! 'Tis the spiriters come back! Stop them! Run, bairns, run! Sparple!' But the spiriters had pistols and shot over their heads, so they feared to come close." He pulled up a trouser leg to show wheals from the whips, still red and unhealed.

Jamie was dazed. It was like a tale from the Dark Ages—or an old wives' tale to make small children mistrust strangers. But here she was. Here they were. And other girls had been stolen. Attercap recounted tale after tale of trickery and woe, and Jamie listened numbly.

It began in September, with dairymaids and farm laborers. Bella, a little dairymaid at a farm near Straloch, hid in a hedge that ran along the farm lane to weep away her homesickness, when a soft voice spoke through the hedge. "Hoots, lassie, it canna be as bad as a' that."

"It *is*." The little dairymaid sobbed. "I wish I were home wi' my six wee brothers and sisters, and all."

"And where is home?" The voice was soft as thistle-down.

"By Whitecairns." The little dairymaid dried her eyes. "Father is a weaver, and Mother and Anne and Geordie is knitters. But when I hold the knitting needles my fingers is all thumbs, they say, so I must go off to be a dairymaid instead." She sobbed again. "I tip over the curds and spill the milk, for my fingers *is* all thumbs."

"Then they must find you better work," the stranger said. "Come, here's a wee hole in the hedge. I will take you home."

The little maid pushed her way through the hedge and smiled up at the tall, whiskered man who stood there. A pretty, bright-eyed ferret sat on the shoulder of his blue coat.

"We'll take the long way to Whitecairns," the man said, "for I have business in Belhelvie."

With each spiriter, the pattern was the same and yet different. In the churchyard at Newmachar, the parson's boy, cutting grass among the gravestones with a sickle, stood up to stretch and saw a stranger at the gate. The man wore a three-cornered hat, and a green silk scarf knotted at his throat, and leaned on a knobbly walking stick. He squinted at the church in puzzlement. "Alas!" he said. "This isna Kinmuck. I fear I've lost my road. Tell me, young sir, will this road take me to Blackburn?" He pointed with his stick southeast along the lane.

"Nay," the boy answered. "'Tis for Aberdeen. But if you'll follow it awhiles, there's a way that turns off toward

Hatton of Fintray and Blackburn." He bent again to his work.

The stranger stepped into the road, tapping his stick from one side to the other. But then he turned back to the gate. "Young sir, might you help me? I'm sand-blind, and fear I'll miss the turning. Would ye see me that far on my road?"

So the parson's boy laid down his sickle and set off at the blind man's side. The stranger held him fast by the elbow, the better to be sure of his footing, and told him tales of the north, where rivers of ice ran down to the sea, and of London Town in the south, where folk lived in houses four and five storeys tall, and great lords and ladies ate roasted swans and pickled peacocks' tongues.

Another stranger sat on a bench outside the tavern at Banchory, a tankard of ale at his hand, and sang songs of the sea, and told tales stranger than he himself. Five big lads out of work and two small ones on their way to fetch a peck of oats and a peck of rye from the farm nearby crowded close to listen and wonder. He sang "Oh, the Ocean Waves Do Roll," and "Blow, Ye Winds, High-ho!" and he told of the sailfish and mermaids that swam in the sea, and of islands made all of ice. He told, too, of marvelous America, where the hills hid boulders of gold, and His Majesty the King gave fifty acres of land to every brave soul who sailed there and stayed. Then the sailor tipped up his tankard, drained off his ale, and wiped his mouth with the back of his hand.

"I'm away, then, friends," said he, "but any who wish to pull up anchor and sail the sea to Virginia are welcome to come wi' me. I'll put in a good word wi' my captain, and *whisht!*, your fortunes are made. You'll be bringing gold guineas home to your mothers."

Of the five tall lads and two small, all but the tallest

and smallest sailed down the road with the stranger, singing, *"And the stormy winds do blow"* to his *"Oh, the ocean waves do roll."*

The tallest watched them go with a sigh, but smiled when he thought of home and the miller's bonny daughter. The smallest struggled home with the sacks of oats and rye, and wept for his brother gone and his mother's tears yet to come.

By the hiring post at Dalgattie Fair, three big girls hugged their arms against the sharp September chill. Shyly, they shook their heads at the "farmer" in the brown coat and high boots.

"I canna pay more," he said. His clothes were dusty, but his watch chain shone gold, his whiskers were neatly trimmed, and under their dust his boots were new.

"Show me your hands," said he, and they did. Two pair were callused and red, the third pink and soft.

"'Tis field-workers I want—but, there! Ma wife has need of a milkmaid, too. I will pay no more for the year but the pound in wages and the pair of shoes, but I'll give ye a gown apiece from the wool of our sheep, and a peck o' meal to carry home at the end."

The three whispered among themselves, then nodded all together.

"Done!" said the stranger, and he gave them a shilling apiece to seal the bargain. They picked up their bundles and followed him from the marketplace out of the town.

And so it went. Strangers slipped along the roads and paths that led down to the River Dee, gentle as ladies, sweet-tongued as minstrels, with smiles like honey. The lads listened to strangers' tales, and fell in at their heels. They swept up Attercap, who was adrift, and had no family. The twos and threes became fours, the fours fives, and they sang as they walked.

In their fives, the boys and girls crossed the Aberdeen road to ford the River Dee. "'Tis only a wee mile or so out of the way," said each stranger, "for I am to meet a friend near Strachan." But as they came to the crossway past Strachan their fives became tens, and the tens thirty, and the songs wavered. The sweet tongues turned sharp, the fine manners grew rough, and the smiles narrowed to slits. Pistols appeared from under coats. Sharp dirks showed at belts, and walking sticks became cudgels.

Like cattle, the children were herded from the path and driven across the hillsides toward the seacoast. Not far south of Aberdeen, they were herded into an abandoned barn and kept there for weeks, fed on turnips and oatmeal. Then, one night the guards took them down to the shore. There, they were hurried into small boats and carried out to the *Sparrowhawk*, anchored a quarter mile off Aberdeen. Here in the hold, they had sat huddled up in the dark, boys and girls together, for two days with little water and no food. With the great swell of the tide, many were seasick despite their empty stomachs.

And then the *Sparrowhawk* waited. Every day after that for a week, the children were ordered up on deck for exercise. Then one morning, the ship suddenly spread her sails.

"It was Mr. Dreghorn, the owners' agent, they waited on," Attercap explained. "Soon as his foot touched the deck, the *Sparrowhawk* gave a stir and lifted up like she thought she could fly."

"Girls," Jamie said suddenly. "Where are the girls?"

A dozen or more hands pointed toward the deck overhead.

"There's only the eleven lassies," explained an older

boy, dark-haired and blue-eyed, with a front tooth missing and a faint whistle to his words. "Mr. Dreghorn had them put in his cabin, and a bed made up for himself in the captain's. 'Twas scandal, he said, to have lads and lasses togither even if we were good as angels. Not when we've only buckets and a wee bit curtain for the necessaries."

Jamie's cheeks flushed. She had not thought about that. For three months, playing the boy had saved her from being Jamesina. But now that seemed a child's game, one that had been played at Amgaldale with private bedrooms and chamber pots and servants. Now that game had thrown her into danger, and the thought of playing it in earnest was almost—exciting. Or it would have been, except for the smell. This world was new, and ugly, and Jamesina's griefs seemed pale and distant. The thought that every morning would begin in embarrassment was as unsettling as Captain Lumsden's threat of a beating. She thought of tidy, sweet-smelling, fussy Mairi with a pang of longing, but then was startled back to the present by a burst of laughter. Someone said, ". . . and didn't he give a mighty curse when he saw us!"

"Who?"

Attercap's eyebrows, arched like upside-down Vs, lifted. "Where did ye drift off to? Mr. Dreghorn is who. The agent come from Glasgow. 'Twas when Mr. Reece, the first mate, opened the hatch to give him a peek at this new deck, that he saw us. He puffed up like an angry wee rabbit and said, 'Captain Lumsden, when we told you there would be space for ye to ship a wee cargo for your own profit, we did no' mean stolen bairns. How dare ye!'"

The boy with the whistle to his words put in, "Crookie—the cook's boy—he told us the captain was in th' spiriting business before ever he was a captain. 'Tis a fine old trade,' says Crookie, 'when the cargo for America don't fill up the hold.'"

"'Old trade'?" Jamie asked blankly. Rumor of "the spiriting business" had not reached the Highlands.

"Aye, I heard of it when I was a wee lad," said the oldest boy, seventeen-year-old Matthew Robertson, with a catch in his voice. "There was a tall house that folk called the Spiriters' House. My daddy said when there was no spirit ship off the harbor to take them, the children were shut up there. 'Twas said the mithers and fathers came crying after them, and were beaten away from the doors. Their bairns were taken by order of the bailiffs, for they were all of them beggars and idle mischief-makers, the guards said."

"But if that was a lie—"

"Oh, 'By order of the bailiffs' was true enough," Attercap said bitterly. "The bailiffs were in on it. Still are. We heard Mr. Dreghorn say the old scandal is awake again. A year ago a man came into the town and had a wee book printed that told how he was stolen from Aberdeen when he was but eight years old, and sold for a bond slave in America. The wee book said straight out 'twas merchants and magistrates of Aberdeen town had owned the ships and paid the press gangs. Mr. Dreghorn heard that folk bought it fast as honey cakes, so the bailiffs locked the poor man up, burnt all his books, made him pay a fine, and banished him from the town."

The boy with the bruise below his eye gave a snort. "Mr. Dreghorn is in a great sweat for fear trouble will come to roost with the new owners."

Jamie tried to speak with an arrogant assurance. "Then he would be a fool not to take us ashore at Glasgow, and send us home."

Bony Skrankie nodded eagerly. "Didn't I say so? Didn't I?"

"Perhaps," Matthew said, but his eyes were bleak.

Attercap grimaced. "I wouldna hold my breath, lassie."

"I won't," Jamie said, and then drew her breath in sharply. *Lassie?*

They were grinning, most of them.

"'Tis no use," Attercap said. "You're a strange lass, for certain, but a lass for sure. A lad, even a softie, may toss his head and put his nose in the air, or sit, or stand with his hands on his hips, but there's a difference in the way of it. And Skrankie was right. Ye do give off a whiff o' soap and lavender. 'Tisn't a laddish smell at all."

"Best to tell Mr. Reece, the first mate," said Matthew, the oldest. "He's not so hard as Mr. Marr."

"In with the girls, ye'll have a turn at a bed," another said wistfully.

Eight-year-old Skrankie began to whine again. "She could stay. She could tell us tales."

"Like his dear auntie," muttered the boy with the bruise under his eye.

"Nay, 'tis best she goes up wi' the girls," Attercap said with a shrug and a shadow of a grin. "Down here she'd be having us wash behind our ears and say our prayers, and sleep head t' toe in rows."

8

THE WEATHER HELD CLEAR, AND THE WIND FAIR. AT midday the boys were ordered up on deck a dozen or so at a time to stretch their arms and legs, and to play makeshift games of shinty made awkward by the space taken up on deck by the capstan, masts, and hatches.

"But where are the clubs?" asked Jamie.

Attercap kept close beside her. "No clubs. There were sticks, but Dickie Jeffers used one to strike a seaman who cuffed wee Cochran on the ear. They whipped Dickie so sore, his back is scabbit still. Now 'tis not a game of shinty, but of feetie. If the ball comes to thee, kick it. I'll keep watch for Mr. Reece."

Jamie watched the islands far off on either side, the Uists on the right, she guessed, and Skye on the left. They did not seem real. The *Sparrowhawk* itself was unreal. But the sour-faced Mr. Marr seemed all too real. She saw him watching—almost hopefully, she thought—for any boy to make an unexpected move.

The boys' ball was a crude one, more round than not,

stitched out of sailcloth, stuffed with oakum, and daubed along its seams with tar to keep them from splitting. Jamie hovered on the edge of the game and watched the ball fly heavily from foot to foot—it had no bounce. When she saw that the object was to get it not across a line but into a leather bucket, she joined in. With the swift approach from behind she had learned in playing shinty with four older brothers, she cut in front of Matthew Robertson to flick the ball out from under his foot. With a flat *thwack!* it arched up and dropped neatly into the bucket.

Even Bruised-Eye joined in the loud *Huzzah!*

Jamie, warm for the first time since she wakened, was still grinning with pleasure when Attercap plucked at her coat sleeve.

"There's Mr. Reece," he whispered, "Wi' his back this way." He pointed. "Between the helmsman and the captain. There, now, he's coming down to tell Mr. Marr to put us belowdecks and have the next lot up. Come along."

Before she could argue, Attercap hurried to catch Mr. Reece at the foot of the steps. A dark, gloomy-looking man with his hat tipped over his eyes, and the grayish-white stock at his neck askew, Mr. Reece looked half asleep on his feet as Attercap talked away at him, but woke to cast a startled look at Jamie. Pointing a finger at her, he gave a jerk of his head to summon her.

She went, reluctantly.

Mr. Reece was tall, but stooped, as if he would rather have been short, or invisible. His voice was sharp. "What's this nonsense? Are ye a he or she, boy?" His eyes were watery with the cold.

Jamie fixed a scowl on Attercap as she answered. "A she, if Master Gordon says so," she said sullenly.

The first mate frowned. "That's fine wool ye're wearing, lass, and French boots. And a silver pin to clip the heather in your bonnet. Wi' your nose so high in the air, I see ye fancy yourself a great Someone. Are ye? *Who* are ye?"

Jamie bit back a proud answer. All this while, the new danger she found herself in had driven the old from her mind. How could she say "Mackenzie of Grudidh"? The captain of the *Sparrowhawk* could make more profit by turning her over to the king's officers in Glasgow than by sending one more housemaid or milkmaid to America. Both were traps. Not knowing which was worse was as frightening as the thought of being caught in either.

Mr. Reece pulled a large, rumpled handkerchief from a deep coat pocket, searched out a cleanish spot, and gave a loud trumpet blow on his nose. Returning the crumpled ball to his pocket, he almost gave her a watery look straight in the eye.

"Wise lass," he said. "If 'twas me in those fine French boots, I'd not make a peep, either, not to our dear captain or Mr. Marr, or to me myself." He tapped the side of his nose with a finger that almost missed it. "If ye can find a way to get word back from Virginia to your friends on this side of the sea, and if those friends have money, why, money makes a fine spoon to stir up the law to see you're sent home. No, not a word to me! I'm safe enough now, but when I'm in drink, I wouldn't trust me wi' a pennyworth o' peas."

With that amazing advice, he ambled back to the stern of the *Sparrowhawk* to speak with the captain, who stood behind the helmsman at the wheel.

An astonished Jamie whispered to Attercap, "But he's drunk as an owl *now,* isn't he?"

A sudden bellow rang out from the captain, "A *lass?* Marr broke the jock's head and brought me th' jinny? Why the blazes is she prinked out in boy's gear, then?" He swiveled around to glare at her.

"Where's Marr? *Mr. Marr!*"

"Here, sir!" The second mate, a thin, sour-faced man, answered from the far side of the deck.

"Marr, you fool, your young gent in boots is a lass! Throw her in the cabin with the others, and send this crop of lads below. *Now,* man!"

Mr. Marr moved swiftly to grasp Jamie's arm and drag her after him. In the dark, narrow passageway between the cabins, he unbarred a door and slung her into a shadowy chamber where the girls, eleven thin, gray shapes, scuttered away in panic.

Jamie picked herself up from the floor and stood by the door with a trembling in her middle like the fluttering of wings. "I will not be afraid," she whispered to herself. "I *will* not."

There still was Glasgow. She had until Glasgow. . . .

9

THE PASSENGER CABIN WAS A WORLD ABOVE THE BOYS' miserable quarters in steerage. Wooden bunks—shelves wide enough for two grown men or women—were fixed along the walls one above the other. Several of the girls were small, so all twelve, including Jamie, could fit into the shelflike bunks meant for eight. In one corner a brown linen curtain hid the "necessary," a bucket in a lidded box. A narrow table folded down from the wall. Best of all, the cabin had two small, square windows in its outer wall, and a high, narrow slit in the deck-side wall—the bulkhead—that let in both air and a little light.

Jamie wavered between a great relief at being out of the stink and darkness of the deck below, and dismay at being shut in with eight red-eyed, sullen lumps and three thin, silent ghosts. When supper—barley boiled up with a few pale rags of salt beef—arrived in a battered cookpot, they ate in silence, and then crept into their beds.

* * *

On the following day the wind held fair, and the *Sparrowhawk* ran before it, sails bellied out. Jamie discovered that by kneeling at the foot of one upper bunk she could see out of the port and watch the Western Isles march south beside them. The other girls perched in silence on the stools and edges of the bottom bed shelves. They watched Jamie out of the corners of their eyes as if they were frightened hens and she a parrot or she-eagle thrust into their coop.

"'Tis like being shut up in a room full of rabbits," she muttered into the silence.

The oldest girl, Elspeth, gave her a sullen stare. The others only shrank more into themselves. The truth, Jamie learned in the days that followed, was that the great world beyond their hills and valleys had proved so huge and harsh that they could take in little of it. After Aberdeen no one had told them anything. They did not go out for exercise at the same time as the boys. The porridge pot and the heavier water and slop buckets were brought and carried away by a stout, grizzled seaman, not the talkative Crookie. No one spoke to them. For fear of the answers, they asked no questions. Jamie began to be fearful that their dread might seep into her own bones.

The first sign that the *Sparrowhawk* had reached the River Clyde came with an earlier than usual bustle on deck, an odd, dim *chunk-thunk*ing, the creak and squeak of the capstan, and, at intervals, a dim rumble and splash in the sea as ballast from the lower hold was dropped overboard to make room for the cargo to come.

For the first time, the others roused a little from their apathy. Two, Jenny and little Bella, came to share

Jamie's watch at the ports as they passed fishing villages and, once, a small town. The *Sparrowhawk* never drew near enough for them to cry out and be heard. The shouting and bustle on deck grew, and, as it had off and on all morning, the sound of hammering rose from belowdecks.

The sound of the cabin door being unbarred startled everyone. The girls were used to being ignored or forgotten in the long stretch between the day's two meals.

It was Mr. Reece who opened the door. "Come along. All of you," he said, not unkindly. "Orders is, you're to clear out of here and go back below. There's passengers to come aboard at Port Glasgow, and these quarters will be theirs. Step quick, now." A swabber, one of the seamen whose job was to keep the decks clean, stood outside the door with bucket and mop.

On deck, Mr. Marr was shouting, "Bowse away!" and, "Furl her up tight!" and men raced to obey. Jamie looked hopefully at the crew. She had not noticed before how rough-looking they were. Most were grim-faced, and as scrawny and filthy as the children. There wasn't one she would dare ask to pass a message to the town officials.

She and Elspeth edged toward the starboard rail to watch as the *Sparrowhawk* approached another small town. Once alongside, it proved to be all port and no town at all. One large building bore the sign CUSTOMS HOUSE, and there were busy warehouses and eight three-masted ships moored along the long, stone quay. On the quay, officials checked cargo papers, workmen shifted boxes and barrels on handcarts, a few idle seamen sat on barrels, and two fantastical gentlemen in fur-lined bright scarlet cloaks paced up and down. They wore curled and powdered wigs and cocked hats, and carried walking sticks with handles that gleamed like gold. Jamie slipped along to the spot where Crookie, the grubby cook's boy, leaned over the topgallant rail to gape at the two grandees.

"Those men—who are they?"

Crookie turned his sly, gap-toothed grin on her. "Them peacocks? Mr. Dreghorn said they're Mr. Bogle an' Mr. Cochrane, 'Tobacco Lords,' they call 'em in Glasgow. Glasgow's the great town over the river and up a ways. They owns the Sparrahawk, and the warehouse yonder wi' the sign of the three green leafs. And ye."

Jamie gave the cook's boy a haughty stare. "'Me'? What of me?"

"Why," he said, as if surprised, "they own ye, too, Princess. Leastways, an arm-and-a-leg share." With a snigger, he whisked away.

"You, girl!" Mr. Reece shouted in his thick, brandied voice. "Come!"

Jamie gave one last look downward and saw the anxious Mr. Dreghorn, the owners' agent, climb from the ship's boat onto the quay and lift his hat to his employers. Then she whirled away toward the hatch and ladder, still trembling with fury at Crookie's taunt, helpless with anger that anyone alive should think he owned her. In the shadows belowdecks, she touched both hands to her face and felt it aflame.

10

ON THE SHADOWY DECK THE BOYS HAD HAD TO THEMselves, the ship's carpenter had built what looked like a livestock pen across the stern end. All the children were shifted into this new enclosure, and a seaman was left to keep an eye on them. The boys milled around the stalls just inside, but the girls made their way into the one furthest from the gate. "How the boys do stink!" Jenny whispered behind her hand.

Matthew, the oldest boy, looked at the chest-high barrier and partitions that penned them in. "'Tisn't for us, this," he said. "'Tis for beasts, like stalls in a barn."

Jamie lingered among the boys to watch the ship's carpenter and several deckhands at work by lantern light at the far end of the deck. They appeared to be closing off the bow end, too, but with a wall that reached all the way to the overhead beams. There was the loading of cargo to watch, as well. Heavy rope nets were lowered by winch through the main-deck hatch and then straight down through the tweendeck hatch under it, into the cavernous bottom hold. The nets held casks and barrels, boxes, and bundles and bales. There were firkins that must have held ale, casks of rum and brandy, and barrels of wine. Barrels labeled HERRING, others of china and glass, and one labeled SOFT SOAP appeared. Crates and wooden boxes of everything from candles and furniture to tobacco pipes and bricks followed them. When the bottom hold was stacked full and its hatch fastened down, the space between the penned-up children and the busy carpenters at the far end came next. Boxes of cheese, writing paper, and tea, rolls of carpeting wrapped up in canvas, and bundles of rolls of linen and silk and cotton cloth were secured between the deck pillars.

"Hoots! Folk must all be rich in Virginia," a wide-eyed Skrankie whispered.

When the carpenter and his helpers had gone, Mr. Marr opened the gate of the pen. "Right, ye lubberly lobcocks, out wi' ye! We've built ye a new palace for'ard—jocks to port, jinnies to starboard." When they hesitated, confused, he roared, "Move forward, ye codshead loobies!" and shoved them along the aisle crowded high on both sides with cargo. "Lads to the left at the far end. Lasses right."

The wall closing off the bow end was slatted rather than solid. The compartment's two "cabins" together were only a little larger than the pen they had just left. In each, a curtain of old sailcloth screened off the buckets of a necessary. The outer doors were fitted with strong hasps for iron padlocks that closed with a heavy *snock!*

Jamie still trembled with anger. "We're not cattle and sheep," she cried. "How can we sit down and do nothing but breathe in and out?" She buried her face in her hands. "Ah, what use are any of you?"

Attercap came to the high, slatted wall between them. "No more than ye," he said sharply. "We must all sit down and do nothing but breathe in and out for now. Once we're in Virginia—"

"Crookie has been there," another boy said. "He says 'tis warm, and the soil so rich, there is no need to till it. You drop a seed and it grows."

Skrankie's reedy voice piped up. "And there's wild fruit and grapes free for the picking."

"And so many rabbits and squirrels and such," another boy added hungrily, "that ye no sooner set a snare than it's sprung. Ye've meat for every meal."

"But it isn't home," Elspeth's voice trembled. "It isn't home."

"'Twon't be so bad," came a thin and breathless voice from the boys' side. "Crookie says the master we're sold to . . . must keep to the law. No beating, he says. That's better than what . . . the law told my old master . . . at home."

"And," tall William added, "masters must give us clothing and money when our time is up. The seamen say the Virginia Colony will give us each fifty acres." He spoke the words "fifty acres" in a hushed voice, in wonder.

Jamie listened in silence and helpless anger. What did such things matter? The ache in her heart was for the heathered hills, for her grandfather and her aunts. For the first time she put her head down on her knees, and wept.

11

THE ANIMALS WERE THE LAST OF THE CARGO TO COME aboard. A large bull, winched up over the deck in a rope sling and lowered into the steerage, came first. A few of the girls watched from between the slats of the wall as he was urged into a stall. The boys could only listen to the bellowing and stomping and curses, because barrels and boxes rose like a second wall a few feet in front of their quarters. The bull was followed, by Elspeth's count, by five cows, two terrified horses, a pair of large, squealing, spotted pigs, four impassive goats, and three cages of chickens.

"Just what we need," Skrankie muttered. "New stinks."

At nightfall, the animals settled down to quiet snufflings and stirrings in the darkness. Many footsteps sounded above, and from the new voices that floated down through the hatches, the children could tell that passengers had come aboard.

Jamie, sitting in the darkness, knew that the few

frayed hopes for freedom she had clung to were gone, and she was adrift alone on dark waters.

The *Sparrowhawk* retraced her passage northward between the Isles and Skye, and up the Minch into the North Atlantic. As long as land was in sight, the children were kept below in the dark. On the fourth night, the cold deepened cruelly, and they were given more blankets—stiff, scratchy ones that felt and smelled as if they had been washed in seawater. Jamie used hers folded as a pillow. Hunger, the smells, and filth had left her little to be proud of, but she hugged to herself one small satisfaction. At least she did not feel the cold as the others did. She shut her ears to their complaints, their daydreams of food, and their longings either for home or a better new world. Her own world was gone. Vanished with her father and brothers. Gone up in smoke like Grudidh House.

Once the *Sparrowhawk* reached the open sea, the winds shifted and blew from the west, slowing the ship, and bringing heavier seas. The *Sparrowhawk*, running close-hauled across the wind, listed and pitched, and many—from the passengers down to the goats—were ill. Even so, the children were brought up on deck, fifteen or so together, to run and jump. The day was too windy for ball games, even if Captain Lumsden had not forbidden them.

"Have to keep the young villains fit and strong," the captain shouted into the ear of Mr. Speck, a passenger on his way out to be manager of Bogle and Cochrane's store in Richmond, Virginia. Mr. Speck looked weaker and less healthy with each rise and fall of the deck.

Because of the wind and the struggle of the

Sparrowhawk to make headway against it, the children were kept out from underfoot in a strip of roped-off deck barely wide enough for two relay teams to run side by side. From time to time the second mate shouted, "Keep moving, there!" but on the shifting deck, in that narrow place, it was not easy. Runners stumbled and fell. The boys struggled to keep to their teams and win. The girls, in their turn, were flung this way and that as the wind turned their petticoats into sails. They could only join hands in a chain and stumble back and forth in a daze. Passengers came out from the cabin from time to time to watch: a tall woman on the youngish side of middle age, two young men, a short, portly man of fifty or so and his short, portly wife. Most of the children were too numb with the cold even to envy the passengers' shawls and scarves, their coats and gloves.

The short, portly woman watched one day for a while, then wrapped her green and rose Kashmir shawl more tightly around the shoulders of her coat, and set off up the stair to the afterdeck, to search out the captain. Mr. Reece was beside her in a moment, to steer her back down.

"Not a good time, Mrs. Moon, ma'am," he shouted over the wind. "What was it you wanted?"

"That boy!" She pointed a gloved finger at the reeling line of runners. "Why is a boy running with the girls?"

"'Tisn't a boy, ma'am." He cupped his hands to keep his words from whipping away. "'Tis a sort of wild, original girl. Or was. She has grown silent of late."

Startled, the woman peered across the deck. "Curious! Such a frozen face. A runaway, was she? Is that why she is sent into bondage?"

"I couldn't say. Something like that," Mr. Reece answered into the wind. "Come, ma'am. Best you return to the cabin. Too rough to be out."

"Very well," Mrs. Moon said at the outer cabinway door. "But send me that odd child tomorrow. Mrs. Speck and I should be able to fit her out in a gown and petticoat."

Mr. Reece shook his head. "Not a good idea. Captain's orders. They're not to mix wi' the passengers." But a glance across at Jamie's pale, set face—*still desperately proud, but too cold and hungry for anger,* he thought—made him add, "No reason I couldn't take 'em to her. But now, do go in, ma'am."

The wind rose higher still and suddenly shifted, coming more from the north. Across the deck, Mr. Marr appeared and herded the girls below. Men scurried to strike the topsails and trim the mainsails. Mr. Reece ordered a seaman to fasten shutters into the square cabin ports. The captain, looking out to windward, saw a heavy squall darkening the sky and lashing the tops of the billows into foam.

Belowdecks, in the dark, some of the younger children screamed as the *Sparrowhawk* checked, and lurched. And some of the not-so-young. The heavy solid hatch covers had been bolted down and covered with canvas, and there was no glimmer of light. The *Sparrowhawk*'s bow dropped out from under the children where they crouched together, so that they floated as lightly on the deck as if they had been feathers. They clutched at each other in terror. Then the bow rose up under them, and they were pressed down as heavily as if their bones were made of lead. In the stern, the bull bellowed, the horses whinnied, and the pigs' squeals rose to shrieks. The noise of the sea and the creaking timbers drowned out the lowing of cows and the cries of the goats and chickens. There was a moment's lull. Then the deck lunged beneath them all, and reared up again.

In the next lull, they heard a faint, far-off call of "Man the yards!" Then the darkness tilted halfway onto its side. The crash of a wave thundered onto the deck above as the *Sparrowhawk* struggled to right herself.

And again. And again.

After an hour, the worst was over. For the rest of the day and into the night, the ship rode across great, wide swells as high as hills, climbing their crests and riding down again. The fright was past, but in the cold and darkness and the smell of seasickness, few slept.

The cold of February at sea was deep and bitter. Some days were clear, many cloudy. There was always a wind. Squalls bore down from the northwest. Often, in clearer weather and a steady sea, a light snow fell.

On days when the children came on deck, the light hurt their eyes because they lived so much in the dark. When they could not be on deck, some—Attercap and Elspeth and one or two of the others—tried to brighten the darkness with stories not of home, but of magic or adventure, of the Red Etin, and of the Princess of the Blue Mountains. Of the Black Bull o' Norroway, and of Kate Crackernuts.

Two thousand miles of stories, to keep their hearts alive. . . .

At first Jamie, in her misery, covered her ears and turned her face to the rough wall, but across the miles the tales became the one last, slender thread between her heart and home, and she listened in greedy silence.

Four children died, three boys and a girl. They wept so long for home that they had no strength left to hold off sickness or the cold. They were buried at sea, with only a prayer spoken by Justice Moon for farewell.

When the *Sparrowhawk* had sailed two thousand miles, she crossed the great bank off Newfoundland and turned toward the south. The captain's calculations of the longitude of their location disagreed with Mr. Reece's, and the ship came near wrecking upon Fisher's Rip, a dangerous shoal off Nantucket. After that the journey was uneventful—until the cry "Land ho!" rang out off the capes of Virginia.

Virginia

1759–60

12

THE CHILDREN WERE ON DECK AS THE *SPARROWHAWK* rounded Cape Charles on the forty-second day out of Glasgow, and sailed into Chesapeake Bay. They lined the rails in eagerness, curiosity, and fear to peer at the distant fringe of green that edged the water.

Jamie leaned her forehead against the topgallant rail and did not look. Did not want to see.

The *Sparrowhawk* anchored at dusk in Hampton Roads and, early the next morning, sailed up the broad James River. Late in the afternoon, she sailed over the mud bank at Harrison's Bar with the high tide. One young gentleman passenger and his baggage left the *Sparrowhawk* at Sherwood Plantation. At dusk the ship rode at anchor in midstream on the wide river.

The next day, while their quarters were being scrubbed down with vinegar and water, the children were to be rowed the mile and a half to the south riverbank to bathe. A listless Jamie waited with the other girls while Mrs. Speck, wife of the Bogle and

Cochrane storekeeper, argued with the captain.

"Indeed, I *shall* go with them! It would be most improper for Mr. Marr to oversee the girls." She gave him a sharp look. "And after all, my husband does represent the *Sparrowhawk*'s owners."

"At least ye'll take two seamen to watch they do not run off," the captain had rumbled.

As the boat drew near the shore, Jamie stared at the river's bank with dull resentment. It was lovely, lined with thickets of trees and shrubs green with new leaves—weeping willows, acacias and almond trees, mountain ashes wound with wild grapevines. Evergreen laurestinas wore their last blooms of winter. It was the edge of springtime, but the water and the air were chilly. As the girls splashed ashore through the cold water, doves rose in a rattle of wings, and rabbits fled. Jamie's eyes saw it all, but she closed her heart to it.

The eleven girls, their ragged gowns blackened with food stains, tar, and grime, stood huddled together, uncertain and unsteady on their feet, and waited to be told what to do. Jamie clutched her boots to her chest, blank-faced, not caring. The bright sky, the ground beneath their feet, the smell of green leaves—all were unreal. The real world lay on the far side of the sea. The lost world.

Mrs. Speck, a tall woman on the edge of middle age, was brisk. "Take off your outer clothes and leave them here," she ordered. "Disgusting things! I shall have the men burn them. Once they're off, go out till the water's waist deep, and play or swim, as ye wish. It will take a good soak to loosen that filth."

As the girls undressed, she said, "I've brought two good lumps of soap. When I call, ye'll come in to strip off your petticoats and shifts and soap yourselves up. Then 'tis back into the river to rinse. Don't fret yourselves about the men," she said, loudly enough for the two seamen to hear at their posts just upriver and down. "They'll turn their backs, or I shall see that they're flogged."

Jamie dropped her patched-together gown and her once-good jacket and shirt onto the heap of discarded clothing, shoved her boots under a bush, and waded into the river in her short shift—and the old tight trousers, since she had no petticoat. At waist deep, she launched herself forward and struck straight out from the bank. She swam a little way, then rolled onto her back to float with her eyes closed. When she opened them, she found herself floating with the current. She trod water for a moment, and then swam the other way, against the current, as far as she dared go. She glimpsed Mrs. Speck shading her eyes with a hand to watch. Rolling over, she closed her eyes and let the river float her back again.

Giving in to the water was delicious. No struggle, no search for escape. Twice—three—four times Jamie swam, a little further each time, and drifted back. Her mind was as empty as the sky overhead, as the broad river and its featureless shores. Sadly, no islands thrust up sharp, blue-gray shoulders against clouds of cream and gray and the color of seawater. No mountains shouldered up to catch and wear golden crowns of sunshine.

All that lay on the far side of the sea.

Jamie choked, then gave a deep, retching cough. A woman's voice exclaimed, "Praise be to God!" The words seemed to come from far off. She raised weakly to her hands and knees and shook her head dazedly. Awkward hands steadied her and helped her to sit. She found herself on the now-muddy riverbank.

"Wicked child!" Mrs. Speck swept up and down the bank, horror-stricken. "'Tis a *dreadful* sin to end one's own life. Praise God ye failed!"

"It was no such thing. 'Twas an accident." That was Elspeth's tart voice.

"Oh, I do hope so," Mrs. Speck said fervently, but she gave Jamie a doubtful look.

"De' thachair?" Raising her head, Jamie looked around her in bewilderment. "What happened?"

"What happened? You—*sank,*" Mrs. Speck said faintly. "You were there. Then you weren't there." She put a hand to her throat in distress.

"I remember." Dazedly, Jamie wrung the water from her matted hair. "It was Donald. I must thank him," she said slowly. "I will ask Father to give him the silver buckle he has asked for."

There was a sudden silence. Jamie, confused, looked from one blank face to another. "Oh!" she said softly. "Oh." Tears welled up, and she rubbed them away with the back of her hand.

"I was thinking of another time," she said numbly. "Before the spiriters came and stole me away."

Mrs. Speck's hand this time fluttered to her mouth. Above it, her eyes were startled. She said nothing for a long, thoughtful moment. Then, spying the ship's boat, a growing speck upon the water, she gave a clap of her hands.

"Quickly! Here in the bundle is a new shift and gown and apron the captain's given each of you. The boat is coming. Dress quickly."

She watched to be sure that the girls chose well as they sorted through the coarse brown linen garments. The girls themselves did not seem to care whether sleeves hung below their hands or skirts dragged upon the ground. Mrs. Speck watched them with troubled eyes, and searched their faces.

Onboard the *Sparrowhawk* a few boys sat on the foredeck, where the boatswain and his scissors busily scissored away, surrounded by an ankle-deep drift of hair. A few hard pulls with a large-toothed wooden comb, a *snick-snack* over the ears and around the neck, and another boy was sent below. When the last was gone, a swabber swept the deck, and the boatswain handed his comb to Elspeth, as the oldest of the girls.

"Ye lasses may comb your own selves, but ye'll do it here under my eye, for I will no' have my comb broke, or lost down in yon dark hole."

Even the boys had yelped under the comb, but for the girls it was far worse. A great many tears were shed before a winter's-worth of tangles were teased out straight. Some tangles, like Jamie's, were so sadly matted that bits had to be scissored away. That meant more tears for some, but not for Jamie. What did it matter? *If you do not care, it does not hurt. If you do not care, nothing hurts.*

The *Sparrowhawk* sailed on upriver. In midafternoon the children knew from the sounds and the shouts up on deck that they had docked. They learned more when Crookie, as soon as the main hatch grating was lifted clear, skittered down the ladder.

"Crookie! Where are we?"

"What's to happen to us?"

In her corner, Jamie turned away and covered her ears.

Crookie's news was scant, but he made the most of it. He climbed onto the barrel of china opposite the boys' door that had become his regular seat, and settled himself.

"This place here is Montgomery's Landing," he told them. "Bogle and Cochrane's storekeeper here just clumb aboard to cast an eye over the goods he sent for. Our captain says he can inspect it on his own wharf, for he's no' welcome belowdecks."

"He'll not want him to see that they keep us in cages," Attercap said bitterly.

"Did he say nothing about selling us?" young Skrankie asked fearfully.

"Not a word," Crookie said. "Save that the big places here only buys Africans nowadays."

He would have said more, but two seamen appeared in the cargo aisle, and one, with a gruff "Off wi' ye, ye miserable wee scouker" gave him a shove off the barrel. The two of them then set to loosening the ropes and props that held that part of the cargo in place.

"Perhaps they mean to take us to a hiring fair," the girl Jenny said nervously as the barrel was rolled away. She darted a look at Jamie in her corner, pale, still, and dark-eyed. "'Tisn't so dreadful, you know. They tell you if they're wanting a dairymaid or serving maid, or the like. If it's work you say you can do, they ask questions to make sure. Then you agree, and you settle."

"Oh, aye," was Attercap's answer from beyond the barrier. "Only, 'twon't be you that settles, but the captain. 'Tis his pocket the silver goes into this time."

"And mine," came Crookie's chortle. He edged back into view around the corner of a large tea chest. "We all have shares. 'Tis so we'll hold our tongues, ye see. Though mine's only a wee one," he added with a grimace.

"Ye foutie rascal," tall William growled. "One day

someone's like to give thy neck a good twist."

Crookie danced back a little just in case William's own long arm might snatch out between the rough boards. "Aye, and I'll think of ye when I'm back in Scotland, ye great looby!"

He did not see the shadow that loomed up behind him. He let out a squawk of surprise and pain as a large hand lifted him off his feet by his hair.

"Come to poke sticks in the poor monkeys' eyes, have you, Cruikshank?" Mr. Marr grinned unpleasantly at the children in their dark cages. "Not wise when Cook is waving a great tillie pan in the air and roaring for ye. The monkeys must have their dinner."

13

Beyond a halt at Wilcox Wharf, where the second young gentleman-passenger left the ship, the *Sparrowhawk* made good time to the narrow stretch at City Point, where she dropped anchor in the James. The captain went ashore and hired a carriage to take him and his cargo papers the twelve miles up the Appomattox River to the Customs House at Petersburg. Late at night the children heard the bump of the ship's boat against the hull at his return, and the captain swearing roundly as he climbed aboard and stumbled to his cabin.

Late or no, captain and *Sparrowhawk* were awake and underway soon after dawn. Beyond City Point and along the fields of Shirley Plantation, the river widened again, then narrowed as it turned first one wide bend, and then another. At the second bend, where the river grew even wider, the *Sparrowhawk* anchored in midstream.

Half an hour later, the captain went ashore in the small boat, and as soon as the boat returned, the

Sparrowhawk moved on. Crookie, lugging the morning oatmeal along the cargo aisle, seemed as lively as ever—even with the black-and-blue mark of the cook's tillie pan on the side of his face—and as full of news.

"Captain's gone off wi' Mr. Marr to Richmond in a hired cart," he announced cheerfully. "He looked fit to burst, for Mr. Justice Moon and his lady hired the only proper carriage to be had, and took their trunks off in it."

Attercap looked up. "Richmond? What's at Richmond?"

Crookie shrugged. "Not much, though 'tis the main port on the river. Old B. and C.'s main store and tobacco warehouses is there. The captain goes by road, for there's so many twists and turns to the river betwixt here and there that the road's a deal shorter. The waters is shoalish, too, so we'll not sail much further." He scuttered out, pursued by questions, and was away and up the ladder before the seaman snapped the padlocks shut.

"I think he doesn't know at all what's to be done wi' us," Elspeth said as she ladled the girls' almost-cold porridge into their bowls. "The crew know him for a sneak. 'Tis likely he knows only the scraps he catches wi' his ear fastened to scuttles and doors."

Attercap was licking the last smear of oatmeal from his shallow bowl when he heard a noise overhead. "Listen! We're stopped again."

The sound was of running feet. A shouted order floated down through the grated hatches. The children listened to the rumble of the anchor chain as it ran out. For the rest of the day, they waited. Dinner—a feast—was oatmeal boiled up with the last of the ship's stores of salt beef and pork, with beautiful, fat onions and parsnips bought at City Point. Captain Lumsden was late onboard again—they heard his hail from the bank—but though the rest of the night was quiet, few slept. Skrankie shivered, and his teeth chattered more than in the winter's cold. A boy called Thin Angus (because only months before, he had been Fat Angus) was quietly sick on his blanket. Bella wept.

Beside her, Jamie stared up in the darkness and closed her heart. *This is not the real you. This is nothing to do with you. . . .*

The first boats arrived at midmorning. Some came from downriver, with planters from Turkey Island and Curl's Neck and the valley of the Appomattox, and others from Bermuda Hundred and Henrico nearby. A Bogle and Cochrane boat came downriver from Richmond, carrying a number of the lesser planters. Three small boats came from further up the James. As soon as the first cry of "Boat coming" rang out, the children were herded up the ladder and made to stand crowded together on one side of the main deck. Mr. and Mrs. Speck watched uneasily from the doorway to the aft cabins.

Mr. Marr divided the children roughly, pushing them into groups: girls who had done household or dairy work, boys who had worked with animals, or as gardeners or in the fields. Coming up behind Jamie, he gave a sharp knuckle blow to her back that made her catch her breath.

"Wake up, ye ninny! 'Tis no time to be catching flies. Quick now—what work have ye done?"

"Tending cattle. A little," she said distantly. "Grooming my horse."

"Oh, aye, *yer* horse!" he mocked. But then he must have remembered the horses on the shore of Loch Gairloch. "Over there wi' ye." He pointed to the first group of boys and gave her a shove. Matthew and

Attercap moved to make room for her. Skrankie and Thin Angus were with them.

Across the quarterdeck, the bo'sun and carpenter set up a table, and a seaman carried two chairs out from the captain's cabin. Captain Lumsden followed with an inkstand and a sheaf of papers, which he weighted down on the table with an iron bolt. Mr. Reece sat down, divided the papers into two piles, and began to write.

At the sound of the first boat coming alongside and the ladder going down, everyone fell silent, even Crookie. They scarcely breathed as the first men came aboard—except for Skrankie, whose breath grew raspy and uneven.

Jamie had tried not to think of what would happen, or of what sort of men would come to live at the edge of a wilderness. She had certainly not expected gentlemen in blue or tobacco-brown frock coats, and hats and brocaded waistcoats edged with wide silk braid. The first two aboard the *Sparrowhawk* were not so absurdly grand as the Tobacco Lords in Port Glasgow, but they would have looked at home on Princes Street in Edinburgh. Some of those who followed them up the ship's ladder had the look of solid, prosperous farmers much like ones the Aberdeenshire children knew. Others were hard-faced men in shabby coats and shapeless shoes.

As they milled around, the captain raised his voice. "Good morning to ye, gentlemen. Some of ye know me. I'm Captain James Lumsden, and I've forty-nine young Scottish servants for ye. Standard bonds. The olders are bound for five years, the youngers till they are twenty-one years of age. These are no sweepings from the towns. Most are plain farmworkers, but there's dairy and milkmaids, plowboys, and—" He turned to Mr. Marr.

"Two gardener's lads, a seamstress, a young female who's cared for horses, and a knitter," Mr. Marr said. There was laughter at "a knitter." Mr. Reece did not look up from his writing.

"A lot of them's young," the captain went on, "but that means you'll have 'em longer and can train 'em up according to your needs. Fifteen English pounds cash money apiece to start, or warrants for nine hundredweight of tobacco. Twelve English pounds or seven hundredweight of tobacco for the little 'uns. I'll have 'em out in lots, skilled ones first, for ye to have choice of."

Jamie, Elspeth, Bella, Jenny, and two other girls, Matthew, Attercap, Skrankie, and three more boys were in the two groups Mr. Marr ordered to the middle of the deck, on either side of the mainmast, with his stick and muttered threats. Bella was so frightened that the two older girls were almost carrying her between them.

Jamie saw Bella's terror, and fought down tears. *Don't struggle, Bella, for you'll drown! Say 'tis all a bad dream.* If it was not a dream, still it was not real. *Say it is not happening. Keep yourself to yourself. Don't look at them!*

For the men were inspecting the girls and boys like cattle. They bid them turn around. Show how thin or firm their arms were. Show their teeth. "Can ye do plain sewing? Dressmaking?" "How d'ye make up a seedbed?" "How d'ye separate curds and whey?" Talking about them in loud voices as if they were not there. The shabby men were loud and their manners coarse, but when faced with the men who looked most prosperous, they held back. The ordinary farmers stepped aside with respectful bows. The two fine gentlemen had come each in his own boat, rowed by African oarsmen. Or so said Crookie, who had, as usual, appeared out of nowhere to whisper tidbits of news. The two great men clearly expected to be given first choice, and were. Men who did not bow or who moved too slowly out of their way were paid with offended, angry looks. Of the two, the shorter was the finer. The lace braid on his hat was wider, the cut of his coat fuller, its cuffs deeper—and the buttons on his cuffs and at the knees of his breeches were silver. He waited until all eyes were upon him before he announced his choices.

"I'll have the seamstress—the one with the dark hair—and the older of the two gardener's boys. The tall dairymaid, too. My housekeeper needs a girl, and that one looks presentable enough. If she's clean enough for a dairy, she'll do for the house once she's taught."

"Please, sir," Elspeth spoke up quickly. She tried to keep her voice steady, but it shook. "May Bella come wi' me to your house? She's little, but she's willing, and no one's sweeter-tempered, nor . . ." The words trailed off as Mr. Marr loomed up behind her.

Captain Lumsden made a hasty bow to the gentleman, and at the same time shot a warning glance in the direction of his second mate. "Begging your pardon for the lass's being so forward, sir, but I could let the little one go at ten pounds, if you've—"

The gentleman shook his head. "I have no need of her, sir, nor of your so-called 'farm workers.' I buy Africans when I need field hands. Come, sir, let us see to the bonds so that I may give you my forty-five pounds and be off."

"Indeed, sir. Mr. Marr?"

The second mate motioned Thin Angus, Elspeth, and Jenny to the ship's ladder. As the girls hesitated, he pulled Bella free of them and thrust her at Jamie. She snatched at Jamie's hand, to cling to it, and Jamie struggled to keep from looking down at her. Matthew, standing nearest, leaned over to whisper nervously, "Would ye no' say 'tis surely a fine country where the farmers are like lairds?"

Like no laird I've seen, Jamie thought. Sir Alexander Mackenzie was a proud man, but as courteous to his stable gillie as he was to the Earl of Cromarty. Looking stolidly in front of her, she muttered, "My grandfather says 'tis a small man who measures himself in other men's eyes."

Matthew's honest, eager face clouded. Perhaps at the thought of his own grandfathers, lost to him. Perhaps because he knew he was grasping for any frail hope. Jamie did not look at him, or at the three young people standing stiff and fearful in the sunlight by the far rail.

Then they were gone, and the second fine gentleman was pointing at Matthew. With him, he chose the five larger boys from another group. A stout farmer pointed out three boys. "And the little one." He pointed abruptly at Bella. "Can you do laundry, child? Or housework?" At Bella's anxious nod, he said, "Good. Then we shall find something for you." Mr. Marr gave her a shove toward the table where the farmer was already opening his purse.

"Go along wi' ye, slowcoach!"

Too late to be a comfort, Jamie reached out a hand but let it fall as Bella stumbled out of reach. Then she was left alone with Attercap and Skrankie until the next group was ordered across the deck to be inspected, quizzed, and prodded. She fixed her eyes on the riverbank treetops, and fought to empty her mind, to fend off the hard, appraising eyes and questions. To float.

The shabbier men were more alarming, some so gaunt and hungry-looking that it seemed unlikely their purses would hold more than pennies and shillings. When only two buyers and five of the children were left, Captain Lumsden knocked their prices down to ten, and then to seven pounds.

"All bones. Too weak," one man said as he passed by Attercap, and then Skrankie. He shook his head at Jamie with a "No thank'ee; a sullen lass is trouble brewing," and settled for one of the two other boys. The last man took the second boy, and soon both men and their new servants were over the side and settling themselves in the flatboat below.

On deck, the captain was working himself into a fury. "I've a tobacco inspector and a cargo of hogsheads of tobacco coming downriver from Richmond, and three brats still on my hands. I want my money for 'em, and how in Hades am I to get it?"

The cry came from a seaman sitting high in the shrouds. "Boat coming!"

Ten minutes later, a jaunty young man in a green coat and canary-colored waistcoat climbed aboard. His hat with its rosette of silver lace sat at a tipsy angle, and he carried a riding whip. A dagger with a silver handle hung at his belt.

"Late, eh?" he asked cheerfully. "That's me. Never on time 'less I'm a-horseback." He peered around as if looking for the man in charge. "M' father sent me t' buy up a few of your bondservants. Waste of good money, I say. One good African at forty-five pounds is worth more than three servants at fifteen apiece any day. He's yours f'r life, and he don't wilt so much in the sun. Howsomever, m' father says, 'Go,' an' I come."

Catching himself in a stumble, he swept off his hat and finished it up as a graceful bow.

"Chal Leslie of Shaws Plantation, at y'r service."

14

From Richmond, where they were taken by boat, Jamie rode bareback the eighteen miles to Shaws Plantation, with Attercap and Skrankie holding on tightly behind her. Chalmers Leslie led the way on a glossy black stallion so impatient either to run, or be out from under young Mr. Leslie, that it fought the bit and pranced sideways for the first two miles. Even after that, it did not settle down but erupted into a prance at every rabbit or bird or fallen branch. Three Africans followed behind. One rode a tall, bay gelding. The other two came on foot, striding along in silence, then trotting awhile to catch up.

Jamie rode half in a daze, scarcely aware of Skrankie's head lolling against her shoulder. He was asleep. Attercap's bony arms circling her waist held the two of them on. Jamie was lost in the strangeness of being on *land,* of riding. She leaned forward over the chestnut mare's withers to stroke her sleek neck, and lifted her hand to her nose. The forgotten familiar smell of horse made her skin tingle. Almost against her will, she began to look around her.

She did not recognize the flowering dogwood or the trees whose new leaves arched overhead. She did not much care, since they were not willow or rowan, sallow or birch. She would have hated the wildflowers that grew at the edges of woods if she could, for not being yellow iris, or butterfly orchis, or asphodel.

Curiosity did pinch at her. If Attercap and Skrankie had not been at her back, she could have turned for a better look at the African who rode behind her and the two who followed on foot. The two were barefoot and wore thin homespun coats over loose shirts and trousers, much like those the boys on the *Sparrowhawk* were given. Not the African on horseback. The others wore their hair close-cropped, but his was long, drawn back, and bound in a queue. Tall and unsmiling, he was dressed in neat, blue footman's livery with a spotless white shirt and fawn-colored waistcoat. He was as straight-backed as if he had an iron poker for a backbone. The Duke of Argyll could not have looked more haughty.

"Blast!"

Chalmers Leslie pulled the black horse up short. The cartwheel track they followed had brought them down into dappled sunshine on the bank of Shaws River, where a narrow flatboat was moored. On the opposite bank a number of buildings stood at the end of a long wharf. A stout gentleman in riding boots and a brown coat and breeches stood talking with another man. When he spied the newcomers on the east bank, he cupped his hands to his mouth and sent an angry shout of, *"Where have you been, you rascal?"* ringing across the water.

The young Mr. Leslie drew a small, silver flask from one deep coat pocket, unscrewed the top, and took a long swallow. "Look smart, boys," he said on returning it to his pocket. "The colonel's in a temper. Jacob, you and Cyrus swim the horses across. The new servants'll come with Royal and me."

Sharply, he ordered the children down off their perch and into the flatboat, where they sat on the thwart in the middle. The tall African took up a pole nearly twice as tall as himself, and stepped over them into the prow of the boat. Chal Leslie sat on the cushioned seat at the back. When they reached midstream, he called out cheerfully to his father, "The fault is all mine, sir! I made Royal dress up and come with me. I should have asked, but a fellow likes to travel in proper style, y'know, and I feared you'd say 'no.' Have I put you in a passion?"

"Indeed, you have, sir! I've been watching for you these past two hours. Did you go by way of Williamsburg to find the *Sparrowhawk*? I was about to send Mollison in search of you."

The tall African poled the boat neatly alongside the wharf and bent to take up the mooring rope. He moved without haste or apparent effort and, with one hand and a deft knot, tied the boat fast to a heavy iron staple fixed into a wooden piling. With one foot on a wharf brace and the other on the boat's gunwale, he gave Chal Leslie a hand to the ladder. As he did so, Jamie saw that his shirt and coat sleeves were too short, and that a deep, puckered scar ringed each wrist.

Colonel Leslie, Chal's father, was a shorter, stouter, more weather-browned version of his son. He looked—except for the fine cloth of his coat and the heavy gold watch chain across his waistcoat—much like any prosperous farmer. He stared as the three children appeared on the wharf, then waved them away toward the road at its end. They stopped not quite out of hearing, beside Jacob and Cyrus, who had come up with the horses. They heard the colonel growl, "What the deuce are *they*, sir?"

The young man swept off his hat. "Why, the bondservants, sir." He reached into a pocket and brought out the papers Mr. Reece had given him. "'Twas the best I could do. When you spoke to the *Sparrowhawk*'s captain at Bogle and Cochrane's in Richmond, did he tell you 'twas a shipload of infants? It was. Vagrants and thieves, most of 'em, I'd guess, but these three was sold by their parents. He guaranteed it."

Jamie stiffened. Attercap's hand shot out to fasten on her wrist, but when she made no move to pull away, he let it go. "They're all three of 'em young," Chal Leslie said, "so we'll have 'em for eight or ten years instead of four."

The man with Colonel Leslie turned on the three a cool glance that seemed to say they were a bad bargain even at that.

The colonel groaned. "Ten years? What good is that? One's a female and can't be worked in the fields with the men and the Africans without our risking a fine. 'Tis illegal. The other two between 'em look as if they haven't the muscle to lift a bag of feathers. By heaven, why *aren't* they field hands? Field hands are what I sent you for. By this day next month I must have hills hoed up for planting twenty thousand seedlings."

"I had no choice, sir. There wasn't but a handful of 'em anywhere near full grown, and those were snapped up before I could wedge a word in."

"Pah! Before you got there, you mean."

"Well, sir, I thought we could call these three a birthday gift for my mother. No, they ain't field hands, but she'll find work for 'em to do around the house."

Jamie turned her head away to shut them all out. Jacob and Cyrus moved the horses to screen themselves from view as they whispered together, stifling grins. The man Royal ignored the scene completely. Head up, he gazed at the puffy white clouds that drifted eastward toward the tidelands and the sea. *And Africa,* Jamie thought, distantly.

The argument that was not quite an argument grew louder by a notch.

"What of the rest of my tobacco notes? They were fifty silver English pounds' worth. Curse it, sir, Boyle and Cochrane is so tight with their credit, I can't be throwing money away on your entertainments."

His son grinned sheepishly. "I confess, sir, I wagered the tobacco notes on the race, but I won. Here is thirty-five in hard money. I must owe you the fifteen for mother's brats."

The colonel pocketed the purse with a snort. "Must you? If you wagered and won, where are your winnings?"

"There, sir." Chal Leslie pointed with his riding whip to the black stallion. "There are my winnings. All two hundred pounds." He strode off the wharf and came to take the bridle from Jacob.

His father stood thunderstruck. "Two hundred pounds for another horse? That's ten or a dozen white field hands or four good Africans! Gad, Chal, you will be the ruin of me! Why can't you take an interest in the planting, like your brother? If this year's crop falls short, or the leaf is poor, or the price falls, Bogle and Cochrane will worry me to death for the ten thousand pounds I owe 'em. Do you *wish* to lose Shaws?"

He suddenly stopped short, seeing Attercap and

Skrankie taking in every word. "You there, Royal, take those three up to the kitchen and leave 'em with Mary. Well?—off with you! Jacob, you and Cyrus take the bay and the chestnut up to the stables."

With a stately nod but not even a look at the children, Royal set off past the warehouse, along a graveled road that curved up across a broad meadow. Behind them, the children heard Chal Leslie assure his father that he was heartily sorry for taking Royal away from his work.

"Best man I have," his father growled, and sighed. "Next time you want to make a show of jaunting around with a manservant, Chal, dress Cyrus up. At least the coat'll fit him."

"Hee-ee!" Jacob laughed aloud as soon as he and Cyrus were out of the colonel's hearing. "You a footman! That devil Mr. Chal, he beat on his daddy like a *dudugudu,* then strum him like a *molo!*"

Jamie stumbled along at Attercap's heels, with Skrankie trailing behind. *Perhaps I am fevered,* she thought. Perhaps it was the strangeness of being treated as if she were invisible. She glanced down at her feet as if unsure that they touched the road with each step. She felt as out of touch with them as if she were numb from the waist down.

She followed blindly.

This is what it is like to be nobody.

15

THE SOUTH FRONT OF THE HOUSE CALLED SHAWS OVERlooked the river from the crest of a broad, grassy slope bordered with woods on either side. A large, square, brick building, it had a steep, hipped roof with attic gables, and a tall chimney on each corner. The panes of the windows on the west side glittered in the late afternoon sun as the children were led past. Even Skrankie, stumbling with weariness and hunger, gazed upward with his mouth open in awe.

On the north side, Shaws had a second entrance, equally fine, that faced a road that rolled away over gentle hills. Two cabins with white-painted siding stood off to each side of the big house, hidden by pines and weeping willow trees. Nearer the house was a larger, taller cabin with a chimney at each end and freshly whitewashed clapboards. Royal raised a long arm to point. "Kitchen," he said, and turned away.

The hens scratching by the doorstep of the high-roofed cabin were too intent upon their search for insects and stray seeds or grain to scuttle aside. The children edged through them to reach the door.

Inside, a stout African woman wearing a blue gown and white apron sat on a low stool beside the great fireplace and stirred the stew in the pot that hung over the cookfire.

She did not hear them at first. By the time she turned, Skrankie had stepped inside and quietly curled up on the floor to sleep. Only stubbornness kept Jamie on her feet. The long, unaccustomed ride and the uphill walk after so long on shipboard had left her sore and trembling. Beside her, Attercap coughed.

"*Alahamdu-lillaahi!*" the woman exclaimed. Then—uncertainly, for Attercap and Jamie stood in the doorway and were silhouetted against the sunlight beyond—she asked, "Who be you?"

"The gentleman—the colonel—sent us," Attercap said. "A man named Royal brought us here."

The woman—she was in late middle age, perhaps older—shook her head in wonder. "*You* be the servants come from across the *baabaa?*" She gave a scornful laugh. "That man! Why he want to buy more white trash? He got too many now. And you be so *domanding*—runty little things, good for nothing but housework. He want men for the fields, not boot shiners and silver polishers."

"*Aleekum-sa-laam,* Mariyaama." The man Jacob appeared behind Jamie and Attercap and gave them a shove on into the room. "It was not the master. It was that foolish *saroo,* Mr. Chal. What for dinner?"

The woman Mariyaama slapped his hand away from the long wooden spoon in the stewpot. "Same as most days. And not for you 'less you a houseman all-a-sudden. You eat later. You have time for fool around, you snare up a rabbit for cookpot in quarter, an' not pester me." Mariyaama turned her back, took up her spoon, and went back to her stirring.

Attercap stood and waited patiently. Jamie's eyes drooped, and flew open only as she was about to drop in a heap on the floor. She stumbled back against the wall beside the door and was sliding down it to sit beside the curled-up Skrankie when another shadow fell across the doorstep.

"Mary? Colonel Leslie wants ham for our supper, so I have fetched one from the attic."

The voice was a young Englishwoman's, but the woman who followed it into the kitchen was middle-aged. Except for being thick-waisted, and wearing her hair too girlishly dressed, she was quite beautiful. She crossed the room and set a cloth-wrapped parcel down on a table. "You must slice the ham as thinly as you can, Mary," she said, "and spread the slices out on the dish like a fan, to make it look like more." She spread her fingers like a fan in the air. As she did so, she turned a little and saw Attercap wavering back and forth on his feet an arm's length away.

"Mary! Whose are these?"

Jacob, who had shrunk into a shadowy corner at her appearance, stepped forward as if he were the official messenger. "They for you, Mist'ess. Mr. Chal, he buyed them for you. Colonel, he say bring them here from little boat."

Mariyaama waved her long spoon. "He did not say it to you, *Junkung Danjoo—Billali Danjoo,*" she scolded. "*Ayi, ayi, ayi,* out of my kitchen!"

Jacob threw her a reproachful look and stayed where he was.

Mrs. Leslie hardly noticed. "For me? How odd!" she

said uncertainly. "I am sure it is very good of him, but . . ." She straightened and took a deep breath. "The colonel or Mr. Chal will explain it to me, I daresay. For now we may as well make use of them. What can they do?"

"The girl, she good with horses," Jacob answered. "Small one, they say he make foot—foot—"

"Stockings. He can knit stockings," Attercap put in. Skrankie had awakened but could manage only to sit up and rest his head upon his knees.

Mrs. Leslie crossed the sanded earth floor and bent down to lift Skrankie's head by the thatch of curls the haircutting boatswain had left on top. Startled by his thin, old-man's face and huge, pale eyes, she let go hastily and stepped back. "Poor wretch," she murmured. "He won't last. Not once summer comes."

To Mariyaama, she said, "Feed this one some soup now, and more again at suppertime. Tomorrow he can take little Hester's post to watch for visitors. I'll send Hester along to Bess. She's old enough now to learn to sew a straight seam." To herself, she muttered, "He'll need a white shirt and some knee breeches—and hose and shoes."

She looked around her. "Where is—oh, there you are, Naomi," she said as a thin African woman in a flowered dress and spotless white apron appeared in the doorway. "Bustle yourself back up to the attic and find a decent shirt and some knee breeches and hose and shoes to fit this one." She pointed to Skrankie. "The big humpbacked trunk has all of Mr. Chal's and Mr. Oliver's old clothes in it, but mind you don't fetch anything fancy."

"Yes'm," the young woman said, and vanished.

Mrs. Leslie nodded toward Skrankie. "You, girl—what does he call himself?"

Jamie had not been listening. Her only answer was a

startled stare. Again it was Attercap who spoke up. "Peter Cochran," he said. "We—everyone on the ship called him Skrankie, for he's such a scraggy, shriveled-up, sickly bit of a thing. But he's still wi' us, though bigger lads sickened to death."

"We will call him Peter," their new mistress said. "We have no Peter. And you, girl, what are you called?"

Attercap slid a worried glance at Jamie. Her lips now were set in a thin line, and her eyes stared vacantly toward the loft overhead. "She's Jamie. 'Tis short for Jamesina. I'm Archibald Gordon—Archie," he added quickly. "But they call me Attercap."

"'Attercap'?" Mrs. Leslie gave him a sharp look. "But that is a word for 'spider,' is it not? A nasty name! Are you so poisonous that you deserve it? You seem mild enough."

"'Tis because he climbs," croaked Skrankie, coming a little to life. "As well's a spider, almost."

"A climber." Mrs. Leslie gave a sour little snort of laughter. "A climber, a stocking-knitter, and a sullen, tongue-tied maid. I must thank my son," she drawled.

She turned to Jacob, listening in the shadows, and was suddenly brisk again. "Jacob, take Archie down to the tobacco storehouse. If he is so good at climbing, perhaps the colonel can use him to bring down the highest racks of the weed."

When they had gone, she stopped on her own way to the door to consider Jamie in silence. The only sounds were of Skrankie's harsh breathing, and of Mariyaama's little shovel scraping on the hearthstones as she scooped hot coals onto the lids of several iron kettle ovens. Perhaps it was the growing aroma of food that quickened Jamie, perhaps the silence, but even in her not-caring she felt a faint prick of curiosity. Turning her head toward the dark shape against the sunlit doorway, she saw the firelight glitter in Mrs. Leslie's eyes as if they were wet with tears.

The voice was hard, though. "Tomorrow will be soon enough to decide whether it's the stables for you, or a needle and thread." Then she was gone.

Mariyaama had seen the tears, too, and Jamie's confusion. "Pay no mind, girl. Tears sparkle pretty, but dry fast. Here, you come, stir me this stew awhiles."

Jamie stirred while Mariyaama unwrapped the half ham and began to cut slices of an astonishing thinness. The fat and scraps went into a frying pan with a dishful of chopped onions while Jamie watched maize kernels and beans make lazy circles in the kettle in the wake of her spoon. A large bone from some earlier ham surfaced now and again, boiled white and clean of every shred of meat.

"Why the tears?" Jamie stirred herself to ask at last.

Mariyaama laughed as the onions sizzled over the fire. She shook the frying pan. "How you think she come to this country? In fine big ship room? Rich folk 'round here, they don't know, but servants, they keeps their ear to the door. The colonel? When he a young man, he a rascal. His fine family pay him stay 'way from England. When he down in Carolina, he see Mist'ess, all young an' tasty an' pretty like a shandy-leer. He gots to have her. She only a nursemaid, but she tell him how her daddy in England be rich, only lose all his money. She make Master marry her all proper. But"—The old woman giggled in delight—"Horatio, down to Wilton, he in Carolina back then with his master. He hear it there. For true, her mama die in London Town. She got no daddy.

In London Town they sweep white trash and little ones with no daddies onto ships an' send 'em here." Her old eyes shone with pleasure, malice, and bitter pride, and she shrugged.

"Like you, girl."

16

Colonel Robert Leslie—he was a colonel in the Virginia militia—sat at his desk in his office, another of the outbuildings at Shaws. The desk, a wide table as brightly polished as the dark oak floor, was inlaid with leather on the top, had a row of shallow drawers along the colonel's side, and curved legs with feet like lion's paws. Mr. Mollison, who was both his secretary and the steward—the manager—of the plantation, sat beside it.

Jamie, Attercap, and Skrankie stood in a ragged row before the desk with as much attention as they could muster. It was not much, for the long weeks of cold, hunger, and fear had overtaken even the stringy-tough, coolheaded Attercap. He trembled with weariness, and his long legs longed to fold up under him. Colonel Leslie frowned at the three of them as if to say that they added up to a very poor bargain indeed.

"Now, then," he began abruptly. "I mean to do right by the three of you, even though by my son's account the captain of the *Sparrowhawk* says you're all runaways or worse, and liars to boot. Firstly: when you were hauled before the magistrates to be placed in bondservice, were you given your bonds, and were they explained to you? Yes, or no?"

Attercap gave Jamie a despairing look and, drawing a deep breath, began, "No, sir, for we—"

The colonel broke in sharply. "I did not ask for reasons, boy, so if you will not say 'yes' or 'no,' I take that as a 'no,' and you may hold your tongue." He made a sign to Mr. Mollison, who produced several papers. "My secretary has taken your names from the receipt my son was given. He has drawn up papers to take their place, and copies for myself. I want no misunderstanding in years to come. In brief, they say—" He read from the top paper, "'*This indenture, made on 7th March, 1759, between Walter Hurt—*.'" He looked at Attercap, Skrankie, and Jamie. "Or Thomas Robinson, or Ruth Grover—*'and Colonel Robert Leslie, of Shaws in Richmond County, Virginia, doth hereby promise and grant . . . for and during the term of five years . . .*'"

"Or," he said, "eight and thirteen for you younger two—"

At the word "thirteen," tears began to slide down Skrankie's thin cheeks. Jamie seemed to see them from far off, and felt dimly sad. Thirteen years, and five for Attercap. Eight for Jamesina-Jamie-Ruth? Eight? Only seven, surely? She had had a birthday in February. . . .

"'*. . . to allow him meat, drink, apparel and lodging, with other necessaries during the said term, and at the end of the said term to pay him, according to the Custom of the Country. In witness . . .*' Etcetera, then your mark."

Colonel Leslie looked up. "It means that when you

are free, I must give each of you three pounds and ten shillings sterling. And there will be no fifty acres from the government. The colony stopped that years ago. D'you understand?

"Speak up, one of you," the colonel snapped. "What don't you understand?"

Attercap answered when he saw that Jamie would not. "'Tis only that—who are they, sir?—this Walter and Thomas and Ruth? They're no' us."

"Not you?" The colonel stared. "What the devil do you mean by that, boy?"

"Only that—only that they're no' our names." Attercap swallowed nervously as the colonel's neck and face flushed an angry red. "My name is Archie Gordon, and the lass is Jamie Mackenzie. The wee one is Peter Cochran."

Colonel Leslie leaned forward. His quiet voice frightened the boys as much as a shout. "I was warned that you were all liars. I will not hear your lies. You were bound into service either by the magistrates or your parents. You wish to return home whether you are wanted there or not, and so of course you will say you were taken by mistake. Stupid boy! A few years' work for a master, and a few more as a freedman here, and you will have a new life. At home you would work another man's soil until you were too old to wield a hoe. Here you have good hope of your own land and no master but yourself. Stop!—do not speak when I bid you be quiet!"

He fixed his glare on Jamie, who was staring blankly at a painting on the wall behind the desk. It showed a middle-aged woman dressed in the style of the 1730s.

"What in blazes ails the girl? Is she ill, or half-witted? Does she understand why she is here?"

"Aye," Attercap said quickly. "She was—ill, and she's no' much for talking now. And Skra—my friend, he's no' very well. Every now and again he hirkles himself down in a corner and chitters away as if we were still up among the icebergs."

"Ague," the colonel said with a brisk nod. "A good dose of cinchona bark, and he'll come right. I'll see to it. For now, make your marks, and be off to your dinners."

Attercap knew he had no choice, so took the pen and made his X on the agreement and copy. He drew Skrankie up to the table after him, and Jamie followed like a sleepwalker. Taking up the pen, she dipped it in the ink and wrote without thinking, *Jamesina Elisabeth Mackenzie.*

The colonel watched in surprise. "The chit can write! That may be useful." But as he turned the paper and read what she had written, his temper flared again. "I said, none of your lies," he snapped. He tore the paper in half and snatched up the copy. Pushing the pen back into Jamie's hand, he guided it with his own to mark a straggly cross in the place for the signature.

"There. There is your indenture, girl. Mollison will make a copy for me, and that is the end of it. Now," he said as Mrs. Leslie appeared in the doorway, "here is your mistress come to show you to your quarters."

To Mrs. Leslie, he said, "I don't know what names they told you, Caroline, but this is Walter, that Thomas, and the girl is Ruth."

Mrs. Leslie smiled and gave a graceful little lift and shiver of her shoulders—as if to shrug off Archie, Peter, and Jamie—and then a nod. "Walter, Thomas, Ruth?" She beckoned to them. "Come along. Colonel, if you and Mr. Mollison will finish your business, I will ring the bell for dinner as soon as I return to the house."

Attercap, last out the door, glanced back quickly as he stepped over the threshold.

Colonel Leslie had picked up the bottom half of the torn piece of paper, and stood staring at it with an uneasy frown.

17

JAMESINA . . . JAMIE . . . RUTH. WHAT DID IT MATTER? A name was something for others to use.

It was not difficult to learn to answer to "Ruth," or to say, "Yes, ma'am," or, "Yes, sir." Or to go where the voices directed. Do what they told. Not to think. The not-thinking was important. Not trying to name and measure each misery. *Float.* Jamie found that she could float through the days at Shaws like a leaf on the river current—except when she was slapped or struck for not paying attention. Then, her eyes flared awake, and she trembled, but since anything she did would earn another slap, or worse, she looked down or away. She said, "Yes, ma'am," or, "Yes, sir." *Wait.* Moving through the days like a sleepwalker, still she saw and heard many things, and her mind stored them away, higgledy-piggledy, as they came.

Shaws Plantation was larger than many, but smaller than the great plantations like Shirley, or Flowerdew Hundred. The house and tobacco storehouse and store down by the wharf all were built of brick in a style that said *My Owner Is a Gentleman of Taste and Wealth.* However, the horse barn, begun in brick, had been finished off in timber. Other structures safely out of sight were built to do their job, and no more. The cattle barn was only a large, roofed pen. The chicken houses and pigpen fence were built of scrap timber and unpeeled poles. The carpenter, cooper, shoemaker, weaver, and blacksmith shared a ramshackle workshop. Only the barns for curing, drying, and packing tobacco were more sturdily built.

The four servants' and house slaves' quarters—one each for men and women—were as crowded as shipboard cabins, with bed platforms along the walls and a second row three feet above them. The difference was in the cleanliness and the straw-filled pallet on each sleeping space. For that, even Jamie was thankful.

The food was decent, though as on the *Sparrowhawk* there never seemed to be enough. Jamie saw, without thinking much about it, that when they had no guests, the Leslie family were served the same plain food on their handsome china dishes. They drank the same brown ale, too, even if it was from fine goblets. In the daytime, Mrs. Leslie and her daughter, Adelaide, who was sixteen, always had their hair prettily dressed in curls, but wore aprons over faded gowns around the house, and slippers sadly down-at-heel. Every weekday morning, they cut flowers in the garden for vases in the parlor, hall, and dining room. Every weekday morning but Thursday, they sat in the sewing circle in the back parlor with Mrs. Mollison, the English servants Alice and Sarah, Jamie-Ruth, Mariyaama's daughter Nyaama, and a middle-aged African woman called Annie, whose real name was Anjila. The cloth they sewed was almost always brown- or oatmeal-colored homespun, woven by

Timothy, one of the English bondservants. The clothes the women stitched away at were plain shirts and trousers, gowns, and aprons for the servants and slaves.

Jamie was given straight seams to sew. It was easy enough: stitch, stitch, stitch, and draw—backstitch, stitch, stitch, stitch, and draw . . . With every stitch the world grew smaller and sharper, and easier to control. Each thread stood apart from the next. Jamie's needle picked its way neatly through them. For the lockstitch that made stronger seams, it pricked down through, and up again six threads further on, then backtracked three threads, and pricked down again. Down through and up, back, down through and up . . . The world was so small that she ruled it. The chatter of the ladies and the "Yes'ms" of the servants faded to a hum no louder than the bees in the shrubbery outside the open window. After the first ten minutes, or twenty, she could draw a deep, silent breath and, with a small shiver, settle into the rhythm of stitches as if it were music. As if the leaping, dipping, bright needle were stitching up a great tear in the world with a cotton thread. And March and April inched past.

Skrankie's upstairs post gave a good, long view out along the road to Richmond. Callers rarely came to Shaws, but when they did, he was to give the alarm.

One morning in early May he spied a far-off coach, and rang the bell that sounded in the back parlor. The ladies hurried to change. The servants rushed to tidy away the sewing. Old Baabukar was roused from his doze in the sun beside the back door. And Mariyaama was warned to have biscuits and coffee ready in ten minutes. When the callers drew up before the north portico, the household was ready. Skrankie, no longer a sniffling parcel of skin and bones, but a quite respectable small footman in white gloves, breeches, shirt, and waistcoat remade to fit him, stood waiting to fold down the carriage step. On the portico steps, the elderly African butler bowed them in through the door and announced them. The Leslie ladies sat in the front parlor in crisp gowns in the latest London fashion, and stitched at a pattern of roses on the embroidery frame that stood between them. Exactly ten minutes later, Nyaama slipped in, carrying a large silver tray with a silver coffee service, cups and saucers, and a plate of thin sugar biscuits.

On her return to the kitchen, Nyaama put her head in at the back parlor just as a patter of rain struck the windows. "Ruth, girl, why you still here? You still sewing? If Missis catch you in them poor-folks' clothes when company be here, pretty soon you wish that *dandang kuruntoo*—that kidnabber man—eat you bones and all 'fore you come here. You come with me. You hear?"

Jamie folded her sewing, left it with the others in the cherrywood chest in the corner, and followed Nyaama out into a shower of rain.

"This here's a 'season'—a planting rain," Nyaama said. "You go 'long fields over Flatstone Creek way." She pointed. "You find that Royal there, maybe Mr. Mollison. Ask them tell you what to do." She sniffed. "White women not 'sposed to do fieldwork, but they put our bitty li'l chil'ren to it, so 'twon't hurt you till noon."

The fields beyond the south wood rolled toward the creek like brown linen bedspreads covered from hem to hem with neat brown rows of little tufts. The figures of men, women, and children moved bent-backed among the tufts at the far corner. At the near corner, these could be seen to be neat, almost knee-high hills, spaced three to four feet apart, each flattened a little at the top to take the young tobacco plants. Jamie, following one long row, seemed to see it all from somewhere outside herself, overhead, as if she were a gull soaring, seeing one more figure moving into place on the patterned field. . . .

The showers grew into a steady rain, and the rain into a downpour as the day wore on.

Colonel Leslie, delighted to have perfect weather for planting, called for his horse and his younger son, Oliver, and left Mrs. Leslie and her rain-marooned callers to their genteel lunch. Out in the fields, he shared in his workers' bread and beef and ale, and the jug of coffee sent out to Mr. Mollison, and then he was everywhere. He peered into the baskets of tobacco seedlings with dollar-sized leaves that small black children lugged at a run from one earth hill to the next. He had a sharp word or a sharper smack for any who did not drop the seedling exactly on the flattened top of the hill. He watched the expert planters, men and women, pick up the slender plants in one hand, make a hole in the center of the hill with two fingers, place the little plant upright, and press the wet earth firmly around it. If he saw one not set firmly enough to stand against the rain, the servant was paid with a curse, the slave with a taste of his riding whip.

After an hour of this entertainment, happy but uncomfortably aware of the water that had leaked into his boots, the colonel, followed by Oliver and Mr. Mollison, mounted up and rode back to a bath and dry clothing. Everyone breathed more easily: slaves, servants, overseers, and Royal, who interpreted for the Africans who spoke little or no English. The workers fell back into the hard rhythm set by the overseers.

Jamie was forgotten at the house after the noon meal. She worked on with the little children, hurrying back and forth from the seedbeds with basketsful of fresh seedlings. Trotting barefoot along the muddy rows. Dealing out to each hill its scrap of green.

The rain let up at suppertime, but in the morning fell steadily again. As always, the slaves and servants were up before six to light fires and cookfires and go about their work. Nothing stopped for the rain. At midday the sky began to threaten better weather, and all of the household servants but Skrankie, Mariyaama, Nyaama, and the two ladies' maids were ordered out to the planting fields. The next morning when the sun rose in a clear sky, Jamie was not the only one to creep stiffly out of the servants' quarters, or to stifle sneezes. The stiffness did not last, and helping to sow a row of tobacco became as mindless as sewing a seam.

After planting season, Mrs. Leslie ordered Nyaama to find "Ruth" an apron and ruffled cap, and an oatmeal-colored gown of finer linen than the one that Captain Lumsden had provided. She then set out to teach her to set table and serve at dinner. Baabukar—Old Bob—had too unsteady a hand to serve, and the colonel grumbled that Nyaama was too brisk.

"A gentleman don't want to be hurried from his soup right through to his pudding," he complained. "That Naomi whisks the china away 'fore my fork makes it down to the dish. She brings the sauce or th' port before I can open my mouth to ask for it. It ain't genteel."

Mrs. Leslie was both pleased and puzzled to see that the girl Ruth knew where each of the forks and knives and goblets should go. She knew from which side to serve food, and to remove plates. At dinner she carried the soup tureen from the kitchen to the handsome new

London sideboard, but then had to be reminded to serve the soup it held. She waited obediently outside the open door while Colonel Leslie ate heartily and grumbled at His Majesty's Government for forcing Virginians to plant tobacco instead of a profitable crop, like wheat, that took far fewer workers.

"Curse 'em, it's buy more slaves or be ruined!" he complained as he banged down his knife and fork. Jamie heard none of it. With each course, she had to be told to stop dreaming and remove the plates to the kitchen. To serve the chicken fricassee. To pour ale and offer bread around the table. To remove the plates . . .

"Something wrong there," Colonel Leslie grumbled as the last plates went out the door. "Better have Naomi back."

After dinner, as he sat at the table with his two sons, the colonel stroked his chin and confided to them a piece of news from Richmond.

"Rumor is," he said, "that sea captain fellow you bought those three youngsters off of, Chal, is a spiriter. I heard Bogle and Cochrane mean to get rid of him once he docks in Glasgow. Thing is, sooner or later we must have Justice Moon and his lady to dine here again. Can't put it off too long. But, you see, they sailed home on the *Sparrowhawk*, so he may know the whole tale, and he's a magistrate. It ain't that I don't want to do the right thing, and send the brats home, but I don't care to lose my fifteen pounds. Chal's fifteen pounds, I mean," he added sourly.

Young Oliver shrugged. "If we mind our tongues and keep 'em out of sight, who's to know?"

Chal yawned. "Why risk it? Just sell 'em off."

18

For a while nothing changed, except that Nyaama went back to serving the Leslies' meals, and Jamie to sewing and doing odd jobs. For weeks, she and Attercap and Skrankie saw nothing of each other except at morning and evening meals, which in good weather were shared by the men and women servants. The men carried the benches and trestles and tabletops out to set them up between the two cabins. The women brought the ale and corn bread and soup kettle from Mariyaama's kitchen, where the house slaves ate.

The bondservants did not talk over their meals. They hardly dared to. Mr. Tompkins, the blacksmith, and Mr. Garsey, the carpenter, had such prodigious appetites that the smaller men and the women and children had to dig in quickly or risk going to their beds half-empty.

After dinner, the men sat at one table, took out their pipes, and smoked. The women brought out their mending and stitched away at torn aprons and worn cuffs until the dusk grew too thick for threading needles.

Sometimes the men bet on the beetle races the boys set going along the tabletop—or on horses if there was to be a race after the monthly county court session. Often they spun daydreams of the land they would buy and the crops they would raise once they were their own masters.

One evening Attercap and Skrankie went to sit on a bench in the orchard beyond the cabins to be away from the others. There they talked of home, and told each other tales of the colonel's fussing, and of his wife's desperate penny-pinching.

Attercap smothered a hoot of laughter. "Today we packed the last year's crop. The colonel never saw, nor the foreman neither, but there was a great dead rat prized in wi' the tobacco leaves in one hogshead. 'Twas laid in wi' the leaves, and more over it. Then on went the cover, the prizing beam was set, the weights laid on, and *squish!* When the cover came up for more leaves to be laid in and pressed down, there was no' a sign of it. 'Twas the little African, Njundu—him they call Junior—that did the deed, wi' his wee innocent face all a-shine like a black angel's—the wicked, lovely lad!"

Skrankie sniggered, and stole a quick look at Jamie. She had drifted after them, but sat down apart, with her back against the trunk of a peach tree. She must have heard, but did not show even a twitch of a smile.

"I think her heart's broke," Skrankie whispered solemnly. "Like some on the *Sparrowhawk*. D'ye think she'll shrink to her bones an' die?"

"No!" Attercap spoke with more confidence than he felt. "The lass eats. She's only—bumbazed. She'll wake out of it. Ye'll see she will."

Because the colonel was short of field hands, as June

went on Jamie was given odd jobs wherever she could free a man or woman for heavier work. Skrankie was sent with Attercap into the fields, and a delighted small black Hester returned to the comfort of the upstairs watchpost for callers.

The three field crews, white men and boys, African women, and African men and boys, each with its own overseer, moved along the rows of hills with hoes, clearing weeds. A lame African was flogged for lagging. In the heat of the day, a bondman cursed the foreman who ordered him not to wait for the water bucket, but to work on. He, too, was whipped, but with half the strokes, and not such hard ones. Both sights terrified the boys. The law forbade a master to punish a white man severely without permission of the magistrates, but that was little comfort to poor Skrankie. Dazed by the heat, he stumbled through each day in terror. Attercap, whose wits had always helped him to make the best out of bad luck, now found them no help. They seemed to have simmered away in the cruel summer heat.

Once the tobacco plants were topped to force the lower leaves to grow larger, the children in the fields had to pinch out suckers so that all the growth would go to the leaves. It was easier work than hoeing. On the hottest days, men dropped in the cruel heat. Some died—most often a Scot or Englishman new to a hot climate. The Africans staggered under the heat and Overseer Biggs's whip. Old Baabukar, long ago crippled by field work, sometimes pointed to the smoke rising from his own or another man's tobacco pipe, and sighed. "There go dead man ghost."

Jamie, banished from the big house, found herself—often all in the same day—cook's maid, messenger, laundry maid, and horse groom. The stable boy Dancer—Dansaa was his African name—did not want her there. When she was sent to help him, he would say, "You go 'way," or would bring a horse out of the stables and tie him to a fence or tree for her to comb and brush. But then the colonel ordered Dansaa into the fields, and Jamie was left to feed and groom the seven saddle horses and four coach horses, and clean their stalls.

On the first morning, the smell of horse piss and hot dung that greeted her on the threshold of the stable startled her awake. A purple dazzle struck her eyes as she stepped from the sun's glare into the steamy shadows. For a moment Virginia vanished, and she was in her father's stable in Glen Grudidh on a hot summer's morning. Then the dazzle faded. The shadows grew shapes and edges. The pain was as sharp and deep as a wound to the heart, but it pricked her a little further awake. She remembered a long-ago time when she took her brother Rorie's dare and climbed the stable roof, and fell. "Be glad it hurts, you little goose," her father said as he pressed a thumb to her forehead to stop its bleeding. "It means that you are alive."

It means you are alive. . . .

Jamie took up a horse brush and slowly began work. She found herself wondering whether Dansaa were Mariyaama's son and Nyaama's brother. He had high cheekbones, and something of Mariyaama's suspicious "I-got-my-eye-on-you" look in his long eyes. But Jamie did not want to wonder. Or care that now he was slaving in the fields. She wanted the warm darkness of the barn to be a world to itself, strong enough to shut out the bright sky and fierce heat of Virginia. She moved from stall to stall, dragging with her a wooden box to stand on, so that she could reach the horses' rumps and backs more easily.

As summer staggered on, the horses became more than names to her. She knew the impatient nicker that sounded even before she reached the barn was Midnight. If she did not groom him first, he fastened his teeth on her thin shoulder when she passed, to give her a shake. Dido always nuzzled her apron pocket for the carrot that might be there, and nudged until she got a bit of it. Hickory, older and more patient, dropped his head to stand with his forehead pressed against her chest until her hand went to the pocket. Chal Leslie's chestnut mare, the one Jamie had ridden to Shaws from the James River, had bright eyes, a nose a little arched, slender ears, and a thick mane, and had been captured wild. She flinched at each touch of the brush. Twice she tried to escape home to the mountains—"Indian country," the Virginians called it. Each time she was cruelly beaten. The third time, Jamie was in the paddock when the mare was brought back. Chal, in a rage, struck with his whip again and again at her head and shoulders. The mare screamed, and Jamie fled into the barn and wept.

She had not wept for the deaths on the *Sparrowhawk*. She had not wept for Bella's terror or for the Africans flogged in the fields. She wept for the pretty bay mare.

Be glad it hurts. It means you are alive.

It was as if Jamie had wakened from sleepwalking into harsh daylight. The barn smells seemed more vivid, the fields greener. The heat was more oppressive, the work more wearying.

That evening she finished her corn bread and stew, and for the first time went back to the kettle at the head of the trestle table to ask for more. The dairymaid Sarah, usually stingy, dished out a generous ladleful in surprise.

It was not enough. She was still hungry. After supper, in the evening heat, in a breeze that barely stirred, she wandered out through the peach tree orchard. At its far edge, she met a wisp of aroma that pricked sharply at her memory. It was there, and then not there. Like a puppy, she turned blindly, sniffing, nose in the air, and stumbled back through the tussocky grass to find it again.

Meat. Game birds. And hare. No—here it would be rabbit, not hare. Stewed vegetables. Parsnips, onions, and potatoes . . .

When she caught the savory wisp of scent again, she followed where it drew her until she came to the path along the rail fence that edged Shaws Wood. The delicious smell came from the field slaves' quarters, out between the corner of the wood and the tobacco field beyond. She would not be welcome there. But hunger and a new curiosity drew her on.

The quarters, three ramshackle cabins with roofs that sagged in the middle and no doors in their doorways, were built in a row along the edge of the wood. Above the door and window openings, awnings of cane lashed together with strips of peeled willow bark gave a frail protection against sun and weather. A cookfire blazed in a firepit at the center of the open space before the cabins. Jamie padded through a corner of the wood and out again behind the cabins. She slipped between the first two to peer out at the clearing.

The Africans and their children sat at the edge of the firelight. They sat on the ground, or on benches or stools made from split logs, flat side up, fitted with four crude legs. At the center of the circle cookpots simmered atop the coals, stirred by Mariyaama and one of the woman field workers. It seemed to Jamie that several of the older Africans who sat on the stools, Baabukar among them, were wrapped in shadows of a lost, remembered authority and power, like invisible cloaks.

"Lu ñoo reere—beeroo?" someone called out to the cooks.

The second cook laughed. *"Ceebu jën,* you calls it. *A tuta domanding, m'parata."* To the children who came to look over her shoulder, she said, "Catfish an' sturgeon an' gar, you see? An' the snapper turtle you bring me."

Mariyaama rose, dipped a gourd ladle into a cookpot, poured its contents into a bowl, and carried the bowl to old Baabukar. *"Aleekum-sa-laam, Mansa Amadu,"* she said with a bow, and then turned to the others.

"*Kaay lekk.* Come and eat."

Jamie shrank back into the deepest shadow and crouched down with her back against a cabin wall to watch and listen. Suddenly more tired than hungry, she was on the edge of toppling over into sleep when a soft but chilly voice spoke almost in her ear.

"This is not your place, girl."

19

STARTLED, JAMIE'S EYES FLEW OPEN TO MEET ROYAL'S cold gaze. She pushed herself to her feet, but he still stooped over her, a dark, slender shadow oddly like the elegant, long-legged little blue herons that stepped thoughtfully along the shallows of Shaws River. Here, away from the big house, he wore a blue turban and sash. A glimmer of firelight shone on the side of his face that he always seemed to turn away, and she saw that it had been deeply pitted by smallpox.

"And is it your place?" she asked sullenly. He always seemed to hold himself apart from the other Africans.

Royal looked away, and answered with a shrug, "*Nandudi lebe nastdata gasde.* 'Those who have the same fur enter the same hole.' You English say, 'Birds of a feather fly together.'"

"I am Scottish," Jamie said quickly. "Not English."

"And I Fulani, not Mandingo, like most of these." He turned to nod toward the firelight. As he did so, he saw that her eyes glistened. "Why do you weep?"

Jamie struggled to retreat into the silence that had protected her for so long, but she could not. The angry words burst out. "Because *they* can still laugh. Because my mother and father and brothers are dead. Because of the ocean between me and my grandfather and aunts and all!"

Royal frowned. "You mew like a sick little cat. Even though you are only a girl, it is not fitting. You will be free when you are a woman. These people will still be slaves in a strange land. I, Diai, son of Joumiko Boukari, I too will be free one day. I am sure of it. These others are Mandingo, most of them, but I am a Fula of the Fula-Futa. My father is prince of men, and master of many cattle and slaves. My clan is great in the lands at the headwaters of the River Gambia."

Stung as much by his courtesy as his pride, Jamie straightened and said, almost as formally, "And I am granddaughter to Roderick Mackenzie, who is master of many cattle, and tacksman and kinsman of Sir Alexander Mackenzie, laird of Gairloch."

"That is reason for pride, not weeping. What reason have you to weep?"

Jamie thought it a very odd question. "Because," she said in a rush of angry self-pity, "I was stolen away. Because I wish to be there, and not here!"

He looked over her head and the roof of the ramshackle cabin to the evening sky's pale darkness and first few stars.

"So. You hear these Mandingos and Jolofs tease and make jokes at each other—jokes that by their agreement, the *sanawuyaa,* each must take in good humor—you hear this, and you think they do not weep in their hearts? Yes, a few were slaves even in The Gambia, and sold by their masters to the English. Some were taken in war by their enemies. But others at Shaws came here together. Their village was raided at night by the king of Barsally, who ruled them. He sold as many as were needed to pay for the guns and brandy he wished to buy from the white men at Fort James, who are greedy for slaves. Do you think their hearts do not weep? Or I? I, who went to the great River Gambia to buy for my father a fine English rifle from the captain of the ship at Fort James—I, who was careless on my journey home, and was captured by two Mandingo and sold to that very ship captain. Of course, he bought me." Royal shrugged. "*Purdi toggore fouru.* The hyena's coat is gray. He cannot change it. And so I am here. And does not my heart weep?"

He asked his question serenely, but his dark eyes were full of pain. For answer Jamie only turned to rest her forehead against the rough wood of the cabin's wall, and pour out the rest of her own tale.

"It was so—there were fifty—over fifty of us. All crowded in. Like sheep. They fed us slops. And we—we had to sleep on the hard deck so close, we couldn't turn or go to the b-buckets. And when they emptied the buckets, the stink was still there. My grandfather takes better care of his cattle and sheep!" She turned a tear-stained face to Royal's handsome, half-averted one. "When some of us died, they sewed us up in a bit of old sailcloth and threw us in the ocean with hardly a prayer. Only, 'Almighty, we send this body to the deep.'"

Royal's voice still was soft, but there was anger in it. "You are a child. You feel nothing of any pains but your own. Those pains are real, but tell me this. Were you used as a beast of burden and driven with whips to the ships? Were you tied neck-to-neck to he who was in front and she who came behind?"

Jamie felt his scorn, and flushed. "The others—they

were driven like cattle. With whips," she said.

"Yes? And perhaps the bad food was much the same," he said more calmly. "But were they shackled hand and foot and chained together in twos? And were there packers—men to pack you so tightly on the deck and the sleeping shelves above it that you could not turn unless all turned with you? Had you scarcely room to raise your head? Did you have need to rise in the night, and have to force he who was chained to you to follow? And did those you rolled over or trampled on your way curse or claw at you, or bite at your feet or legs?"

Jamie winced away.

"When you were taken up onto the open deck to dance the stiffness from your limbs, did many of you struggle to leap into the sea so that their souls could return home? Did many more die in the night because their hearts were broken?"

Jamie could only shake her head "No" as she dried her tears.

Royal gave a graceful, weary shrug. "Then you may say you have been fortunate. And still are. And will be again. Indeed," he added after a moment with an odd note in his voice. "A thought has come to me. Can you read and write?"

Jamie nodded, puzzled.

"It is nothing," he said quickly. "Only that I have been thinking of writing a letter. . . . It is not important."

Jamie spoke without thinking. "You can write?"

He was offended. The brief flash of white teeth that had almost grown to a smile vanished. "In Arabic," he said shortly. "In my country I am *Modibbo Diai,* a man of learning." He gave a wave of his hand in the direction of the people gathered on the other side of the cabins. "Among the others, too, Yaaya—the one you call John—

is *afang*, as the Mandingo call a student of the Koran. But we will talk of this no longer. Let us see to first things. You are hungry, *No nyibre wadiri fuh jungo wofata hunduko*. 'Be the world never so dark, the hand will not miss the mouth.'"

Royal motioned her out of the shadows behind the cabins and into the firelight.

The murmur of voices over the bowls of rice and stew fell silent.

"Heraby," Royal said, with a nod.

"Heraby derong," was old Baabukar's reply.

"This child has eaten, but is hungry. Shall I send her away?"

Mariyaama gave Jamie a long look, then sighed and reached for another bowl. "Come, Ruth," she said.

Jamie took a step toward the fire. "Not Ruth—Jamesina," she said.

20

In August, Skrankie died.

It was almost dark as Jamesina crossed the patchy lawn between the peach orchard and the bondservants' quarters. Ahead of her, she saw the glimmer of a lantern bob from the men's to the women's cabins. A man's figure, carrying something in his arms, followed the lantern bearer. As she came near, she saw Attercap standing pale and stiff in the shadows. Burke, the cooper, came back out of the women's cabin and gave a gloomy shake of his head. Colonel Leslie, who held the lamp, spoke sharply.

"Nonsense, man. 'Tis only a touch of the tapeworm. He wants doctoring and women's nursing, not your parsonical prayers. I'll see him right. Now, off with you."

Jamesina followed the colonel into the cabin in which she and the seven older bondwomen lived. Long, narrow shelves set one above the other along the side walls served as beds, and it was on her own straw pallet on a lower one of these that Skrankie had been placed.

He lay whimpering, curled up in a tight ball. Colonel Leslie held up his lantern.

"Move the table aside, girl," he grumbled as Skrankie coughed weakly and moaned. "We'll see what we can do."

He waved a hand over the child's belly. "Now, boy, where down here does it hurt?" he asked briskly.

Skrankie winced away from his hand. In the shadowy cabin his tear-smudged face was as pale as the colonel's shirt. After a moment a small, bony finger traced a shaky line across his middle, just below his navel.

The colonel grunted. "I thought as much."

He drew from his pocket a handful of small packets made of folded paper, with writing on them, and spread them on the table. Calling for a cup of water, he sorted out the two he wanted with an impatient forefinger, and returned the rest to his pocket. The two on the table were labeled, mysteriously, *Mer. dulc. 6 gr.* and *Pil coch. 20 gr.*

"The lad can't weigh more than a bag of feathers," grumbled Colonel Leslie. He unfolded one paper and tapped some of the powder it contained into the cup of water, and then did the same with the other. "I'll give him only half the dose," he said. "If that don't work, I'll dose him again in the morning. Here, now—none of that!" he snapped as Skrankie turned his face to the wall. "You'll drink every drop, boy, or I must hold your nose and pour it down your gullet. 'Tis nasty stuff, but that's why the worm don't like it."

When he had gone, Skrankie scrabbled weakly with his hands and feet, trying to turn onto his side. The milkmaid Sarah, a stout young woman with strong, pink arms, lifted him easily and turned him. At once, like a pill bug when it is touched, he curled up again into a tight, little ball.

"Auntie," he whimpered. He stuck one thin hand out of the ball. "I want ma auntie."

"Poor little monkey," Sarah murmured.

Out of nowhere, Jamesina thought of Royal's question whether she could read and write. She leaned close to whisper in Skrankie's ear. "Peter? You *will* go home to your auntie. I have been remembering something Mr. Reece said. I shall write a letter to the governor of Virginia to tell him how we were stolen, and that my kinsmen in Scotland know friends of the king. The governor will tell the king, and you will go home to your auntie." She did not know how Virginians sent letters that were not carried by their own messengers, but she could find out. "Skrankie? Do you hear?"

Jamesina dragged a stool across the earthen floor to sit beside him, and took his bony hand in her own. Having taken it, she found herself oddly afraid to let it go. In the oil lamp's wavering light, his eyes, watching her, were large and dark. The shadows at his temples and below his cheekbones showed the shape of his skull. At least his moaning had given way to quiet sighs. The medicine seemed to be helping.

An hour or so later, Jamesina awoke to the sound of hammering, and found herself in her own bed. The oil lamp the colonel had left behind was still alight—or had been lit again. She saw that the other maidservants, too, were stirring, knuckling their eyes and fishing for their shoes with their feet. Sarah was already up and dressed, and pulling her shawl around her shoulders.

"Skrankie—?"

"Gone," Sarah said simply.

Jamesina slipped from the bed shelf and darted to the door in bare feet.

A lantern hung from a bracket beside the men's front door. In the grassy space between the cabins, the table planks had been taken down, and the trestles moved closer together. They held a narrow wooden box instead, and Mr. Thomas, the carpenter, was nailing on the lid. Attercap watched from nearby, and shivered in the night's heat.

"Poor little rat," Mr. Thomas said with a shake of his head. "Weather like this, they has to be shoveled underground quick. Go put your shoes on, girl. Folk say they worms can get at you up through your feet, so best be safe. Hurry, now. Colonel's on his way."

To Attercap, he said, "I'll wager he's madder'n a sack of bees at losin' a pair of hands, feeble as they was. Howsomever, he'll do the thing up right and proper for the poor little beast, so that neighbors who hear of it can't say he's hard-hearted. These big folk are touchy as snails."

Just before midnight, a young African carrying a lantern set off at the head of a little procession. After him came Thomas and Quince, the stable man, who carried the box between them out through Shaws Wood to the path to the burying ground. They were followed by Colonel Leslie on horseback, and Jamesina, Attercap, Sarah, and several of the house slaves. Where the path passed the track from the field slaves' quarters, old Baabukar came out through the trees on an elderly mule. In his wake came a number of other Africans with torches. A few led sleepy children by the hand.

Even Nyaama seemed surprised to see the field hands. Jamesina and Attercap, coming last among the whites, heard her low chuckle behind them. "The colonel, he see all those, he gon' be surprise they come for little stick boy." Seeing Attercap's tall shape turn toward her, she said, "They come like this for Africans. May be they think to shame Colonel, but Colonel got too big a head to be shame. God, *He* see him put all those poor little scraps to work in fields hot like ovens. *He* not forget."

As the men lowered the little coffin into the ground, the colonel said a short prayer over it with the air of a man whose mind was on more important matters. Next Wednesday's horse race at Herries, perhaps.

Or the lost five hundredweight of tobacco he had paid for Skrankie.

September came, and harvest in October. Then the busy, anxious weeks in the drying and curing barns began. Colonel Leslie began to be so pleased with his crop that he invited the county magistrates and their wives and several dozen of the most important neighbors to dinner and a ball to be held on New Year's Day. "That'll show 'em!" the colonel said when the idea struck him, and he left it to Mrs. Leslie—with no ready money—to produce a dinner and decorations to dazzle the neighborhood. Colonel Leslie then rode out to his tobacco barns.

Mrs. Leslie sighed, and sent her maid Alice with Jacob to Bogle and Cochrane's store in Richmond for fifty dozen wax candles, two new suits of footmen's livery, and lace for new caps for the serving maids. In the week after Christmas she ordered a cow to be butchered, sent Chal and his brother off to shoot a deer, and paid Junior and another of the slaves with cocked hats and good-as-new waistcoats to snare wildfowl for a large pie. Hams and dried fruits came down from the attic. Because the kitchen garden had only cabbages and potatoes to offer, Mrs. Leslie sent Jamesina with three flowered china saucers and a nearly new iron stewpot to trade with Yeesa and Anjila—"Liza" and "Annie"—for yams and beans and peas from the slave quarters' gardens.

On her way, Jamesina met Royal. She had seen him often since the evening she visited the field slaves' quarters, but each time he passed her by at a distance, without a word. If she turned toward him when others were at work nearby, he turned away, and yet she knew he watched her. Now, he began to speak rapidly even before he drew near. His voice was low-pitched but clear.

"I have thought much of my letter," he said. "One day each month—do you know?—there is held a county court. I hear the bondmen say that bondservants have the right to speak to the court if their masters do them wrong. You must write down certain things—the names of the chief of your clan and the great men who are his friends. This will make the judges listen to you. Then when you are free, you will carry to England the letter I shall write, and show it to your king. He will show it to men of learning who will read the Arabic. But I have no paper. You will find me paper."

With a nod, he passed on, but his last words hung in the air behind her. "You will find me paper." How was she to find paper? She could not curtsey and ask their master, "May I have two pieces of paper, please, sir?" There was paper for patterns in the sewing materials in the cupboard in the back parlor. There was probably letter paper in the small desk in the hall upstairs, too, but she had been banished from the house and would be punished if she were found indoors.

Paper . . .

21

ON THE EVENING OF THE NEW YEAR'S DINNER PARTY AND ball, the African house slaves, and several Africans promoted from fieldwork for the evening, set to work in new finery. Four of the English menservants were to attend to the guests' coaches. The three older maidservants were sent to help Mariyaama in the kitchen. Jamesina and Attercap were sent to their quarters.

Jamesina had seen little of Attercap since the night Skrankie died. She had noticed, vaguely, that he had grown taller, and silent—and thinner even than before—but little more than that. She was ashamed at having as good as forgotten him. For she had.

She found him, as usual, in the shadowy orchard. He sat astride a lower limb in a leafless cherry tree, head tilted back and eyes closed, riding somewhere in a dream.

"Where are you off to?" she asked quietly.

"West," he answered, his eyes still shut. "Into the mountains. They are blue—did you know? When the wee doctor who collects plants—Weymiss, his name was—came to dinner at Shaws last week, I sat under the window and listened to his talk. 'Twas all of the fine streams and great trees, and rich, chocolate-colored earth, and the light black loam in the mountain coves. Summers there are no' so hot as here, for 'tis higher. 'Twould be a fine place to be a farmer. But fearful lonely."

"Aye," Jamesina said quickly. "No towns and no villages. No kirk. No fields unless you clear them with your own hands and bent back. No house until you build one, and no memories in it. Would you not rather be riding to Scotland? To Aberdeenshire?"

Attercap's eyes flew open. The tightness in her voice, as much as the name *Aberdeen,* brought his mind down from the mountains, and him down from the tree.

"What is it?" Even in the dusk that filled the orchard, he could see the gleam in her eyes.

"We can go home," Jamesina whispered. "We *can.*" As her mouth formed the words, she could hardly find breath to speak them even in a whisper. Her heart thumped loudly, and she hugged her arms across her chest as if that would keep it quiet. "Sarah, nor Alice nor the men, none of them told us that bondservants can take their masters to court! If we tell the magistrates we were stolen, they can put everything right. Royal told me, and I asked Alice, and 'tis true. Why didn't they tell us?"

Attercap put a hand up to grasp a branch of the cherry tree, as if suddenly he needed to hold on to the real world. "Perhaps," he said slowly, "they were too afeared of the colonel. Perhaps they think 'tis a lie that spiriters took and sold us. And if 'tis true about the court, 'tis no' as easy as all that," he said unhappily. "The colonel is sure to know the magistrates. I would not trust 'em. 'Twas whispered in Aberdeen that some magistrates were part owners in the spiriters' ships. Indeed, Bogle and Cochrane own the *Sparrowhawk*, and they are great folk in Richmond. Who would take our word against great folk?"

"Not only our word. *Other* great folks'," Jamesina said eagerly. "'Tis the way the world works." She repeated to him all that Royal had said to her. "So it wouldn't be our word alone. Not if I wrote down names the governor and the magistrates would know, not only my grandfather's name and Sir Alexander's. They would have to listen, and send to England to learn the truth of it. They *would*."

"They might."

His *they might* was grudging, but sounded as if he knew that they must try.

"But the letter paper," he asked. "Why am *I* to steal it?"

"Because I don't know how," Jamesina confessed. "Or where. We must keep out of the house, and the colonel's office is locked when he is not there."

Attercap closed his eyes for a moment, then grinned. "I know where. And how."

The windows of Shaws House blazed upstairs and down with dozens of candles and their reflections in the gleaming glass and silver and mirrors. Njundu, in new finery, handed guests out of their coaches. A kingly old Baabukar was at the portico to greet each lady and gentleman, and Royal stood in the front hall to announce them to the company.

Cyrus and Jacob drove the Leslie carriage down to the wharf to meet guests who came by boat. Virginian roads were bad at best, and worse in winter, and the owners of even the best-sprung and most fashionable of coaches often preferred the comfort of river travel if they had far to go. Jamesina and Attercap kept watch until Cyrus and Jacob's last trip. Then they made their own way down the hill, keeping to the edge of the woods and out of the moonlight.

Mr. Mollison's office was on the second floor of the warehouse facing the wharf. The warehouse doors were kept locked, but Attercap knew what a passerby never saw. The rear of the building, screened by shrubbery and half a dozen old oak trees, was unfinished. Odds and ends of lumber were scattered about. A heap of sand was piled against the walls. The brickwork was complete, but the window frames and sashes below were unpainted, and those on the floor above were still missing. The upper-storey windows gaped like dark, blind eyes.

Jamesina peered upward. "How will you reach it? Is there a ladder?"

Attercap nodded. "In the warehouse. But I don't need it."

He lifted up the skirt of his too-big coat to show her what he wore wound snugly around his waist and lower chest: a long length of thin rope.

"That's from the stables." Jamesina was startled to see it. "But Mr. Quince and Dansaa sleep there. They will miss it in the morning. How will you . . ."

He grinned. "'Twill be in its place again between one snore and the next. I've a light foot, and Quince is half deaf." He kicked off his shoes and rubbed first his feet, then his hands, in the sand.

A moment later, he had one foot on the sill of the ground-floor window below Mr. Mollison's, and a hand stretched up to the lintel above. The other hand and foot felt for toe- and fingerholds between the bricks of the wall. On the front of the building the bricks had been carefully laid, and the mortar between them carefully smoothed. At the back, the colonel had cared more for speed and saving money, and so in most places the mortar was left to harden where it squeezed out between the bricks. For Attercap, those ridges were as good as a stairway.

"How do you *do* that?" Jamesina called in a whisper as his right hand stretched up again, this time to grasp the brick sill of the office window above.

Attercap stretched out a long, bony leg to make sure of his next move before he answered. "'Twas a stone barn I climbed at home, and another and bigger where I was hired out as a cowherd. My grandmother said 'twas my mother's kitchen's stone chimney I climbed first, before I could walk. I don't remember," he said, suddenly somber at the reminder that his old world was as surely lost to him as the dear ones dead and gone.

Then suddenly, *whisk!* He was over the sill and into the dark room.

Jamesina waited in the shadows under the old oaks, and grew uneasy. What if Colonel Leslie did not attend county court day until spring? Or summer? He was often so anxious about his tobacco that he stayed at home instead, to harry his overseers and coddle his crop. He might not go to court again for months, and she and Attercap could not go without him. A servant was forbidden to leave a plantation without a pass from his master, just as a slave was.

"Sssst!"

Attercap's head and shoulders showed pale against the dark rectangle of the unfinished window. Half a dozen moonlit pieces of paper came swooping and dipping down like swallows.

"Take hold at the bottom!" Attercap called in a whisper when she had snatched up the paper. Jamesina saw the rope slither down like two silvery snakes. He had looped its middle around something above, and dropped the two ends together. Jamesina folded the paper in half, tucked it into her apron pocket, and hurried to catch up the ends of the rope. As she stepped away to the side, Attercap came down hand over hand as neatly and easily as if he were taking a moonlight stroll. At the bottom, he took the rope, gave one end a few flicks, and pulled it free. Coiling it back around his middle, he followed her through the shrubs beyond the oak trees onto the grassy slope.

They were only a short way uphill toward the house when the rumble and crunch of iron-shod wheels on gravel sent them flying back toward the nearest shrubbery. From its shelter, they saw the gleam of two carriage lamps move along the top of the drive.

"Someone leaving early," Jamesina whispered as the carriage curved its way down the slope toward them. "Someone who doesn't care for dancing."

The horses and carriage whirled past. Jamesina drew her breath in sharply and half rose, but Attercap's hand fastened on her wrist, and he pulled her down.

"But it was the Moons!" she protested when they had passed. "From the *Sparrowhawk*. Didn't you see?"

"I saw. But what are they to us? They might have seen you, and what then?"

Jamesina stared after the carriage as it swung out of sight past the lantern post at the corner of the warehouse, where the road ran along the riverbank to the wharf. "You're right. It's not time yet."

"Not time?" Attercap gave her a sharp, puzzled look.

When Jamesina turned toward him, he saw her eyes glint in the moonlight. "Don't you remember? Crookie called him 'Justice Moon.' He's a justice. A magistrate. If he is here, they are neighbors. He must be a justice in this county! She gave me a gown, and spoke kindly. They must be good people, surely."

Attercap gave a snort. "'Good' and a magistrate?"

In the ballroom, dancers bowed and circled in a minuet accompanied by a trio of string musicians. Colonel Leslie and Mr. Mollison stood in the doorway between the library and ballroom, and beamed on them. The colonel thought his daughter looked famously pretty. Without turning, he spoke to Mr. Mollison, who stood a little behind him.

"You heard Justice Moon's news from Glasgow about Captain Lumsden of the *Sparrowhawk*?"

"A part of it—that Bogle and Cochrane have dismissed him. No more."

The colonel smiled proudly as his wife swept up the line of dancers with the owner of Wilton Plantation. "There is more," he said grimly through his smile. "Moon was telling me. It seems Lumsden was some years in the kidnapping trade. A spiriter. Once a villain, always a villain. Bogle and Cochrane learned that he and his men set out to capture one last cargo of youngsters, and had 'em onboard when the Moons sailed from Glasgow. Lumsden claimed the older ones indentured themselves for the passage money, and the parents sold away the young ones."

Mr. Mollison tapped his teeth with his pipestem. "The *Sparrowhawk*—wasn't it off her that Mr. Chal bought young Hurt and the girl, and the little fellow who died?"

"Just so." The colonel motioned Mr. Mollison into the library and closed the door. "So I'm to lose the price I paid for 'em, and in the bargain be embarrassed in front of all the county. I knew the brats had no indentures. I knew Moon must've seen 'em onboard ship, too, so I've kept 'em out of sight. What am I to do now?"

Mr. Mollison considered. "Biggs's term is up next month, is it not?"

The colonel nodded.

"Well, sir, I hear his boys have jumped the gun and cleared a good half of the acres you promised to rent him on the up-country property. Biggs'll be out of reach of sheriffs and courts and justices there. Why not give him the boy and girl for part of his freedom dues in place of cash money?"

"Ha!" Colonel Leslie clapped his plantation manager on the shoulder. "So I shall! In fact, add the old cart we don't use, and that mule Old Bob rides, and I needn't pay him a penny in cash."

Mollison nodded. "The 'custom of the country' says you must give him a musket, too, but we can buy a cheap one from Bogle and Cochrane's and have 'em put it on the account."

"Good man!" said the colonel and, hearing the musicians strike up the tune "My Aunt Margery," he strolled out of the library to find a partner for the Virginia Reel.

22

More than a week went by before Jamesina had a chance to pass two of the pieces of paper to Royal. One evening, after another supper that was more bread than stew, Jamesina and Attercap pulled their coats around them and slipped away from the firelight gossip, the mending, and wishful dreams of the quarters, and wandered out to the orchard. They found the tall Fulani waiting for them. He held a small gourd bottle with a long neck and a carved wooden stopper.

"Salamu 'alaikum!" he greeted them. "I have brought ink for you. You have obtained paper?"

Jamesina held out the folded paper, and two goose quills she had pocketed after a fight between a crippled wild goose and the Shaws gander.

"Ink!" she exclaimed. "We did not think of ink when we—when Attercap went for the paper. Where did you find ink?"

"I did not." Royal took the paper and quills, handing over the gourd bottle with a nod as formal as a bow. "I gathered the makings long before I first spoke to you of writing. Pinewood soot, and glue from boiled-up scraps of cowhide. It is not a very good ink, alas. Nyaama brought me lampblack from the lamps of the great house, but not enough, and the glue would be better if it were from ox hides. But it will serve." He held the paper to his breast. "I have written my letter many times in my mind. I go now to copy it onto paper."

He was gone as suddenly as if he were the genie he looked like.

On Sunday afternoon, with Attercap, Jamesina retreated to Shaws Wood and climbed a stout tree well screened by evergreens to write her letters. Attercap held the ink bottle. Jamesina, propped against the trunk on the next branch up, trimmed a goose quill into a pen with a knife borrowed from the kitchen, and dipped it into the ink.

To The Honorable Francis Fauquier, Governor of His Majesty's Colony of Virginia, at Williamsburg, she wrote. Her fingers were awkwardly stiff with the cold. For a land so cruelly hot in summer, Virginia felt almost as cold in winter as the west of Scotland. Thoughts of the fire that burned on the hearth of the bondwomen's cabin helped her to write on, in as few words as would tell the tale. She told of herself and the kidnappings, and the voyage that ended in their being sold into servitude. Then she wrote much the same to Justice Moon, and at the end of both letters, listed her grandfather's name and Sir Alexander's, and the names of Lord Fortrose, Lord Loudon, and Sir James Grant of Grant.

"There!" she said. "That should do it!"

Colonel Leslie did not attend Court Day in January

or February, but spent his time riding back and forth first between the new fields being cleared, and later between the plant patches where young seedlings sprouted under a blanket of straw. He grumbled that the need for new land was as endless as the year's work, for after three tobacco crops a field was fit for nothing but weeds and brush. Jamesina and Atteroap, disappointed, worked and waited. Jamesina kept the letters, Royal's folded inside her own, in a pouch sewn from scraps, which she stitched to the shift she wore under her gown.

In March, the colonel had to go to court. Ned Biggs, an overseer, had come to the end of his period of servitude. He was to become a tenant planter on a parcel of the colonel's land further toward the mountains, and his lease was to be sworn to at law.

Biggs, disliked and distrusted by the English servants, and feared and hated by the Africans, had come to Virginia as a convict. Sentenced in London to fifteen years of servitude, he had ordered his wife to go to the magistrates and sell herself and their two sons, of seven and eight, into servitude to pay for their passage on the selfsame ship. After four years at Shaws, Mrs. Biggs had been free, and was hired as a serving maid at the tavern at Herries. The boys served until they were twenty-one, a year and more ago, and had gone to work "somewhere off West."

On the evening before Court Day, Jamesina was sent to the stables with the colonel's orders to have six horses ready at the north door of Shaws early the next morning: his, his sons', Mr. Mollison's, Midnight, and a bay filly that was to be sold. Mr. Quince and Dansaa were also to harness "Old Bob's" jack mule to the long-unused cart, and have them all at the north door at eight.

"That old rattle-box?" Mr. Quince exclaimed. "'Tisn't

fit to be seen in fine company. Why for?"

Jamesina did not know. She shrugged. "To bring something back? Perhaps he has ordered a harpsichord. Mr. Carpenter says it will be a billiards table, and has wagered sixpence with Mr. Burke. *He* says it will be a cask or two of French wine."

In the end it was none of those things. The day took its first surprising turn at cockcrow, as Jamesina swung her feet out of bed to scrabble for her cold, stiff shoes.

"Ruth?" Nyaama's long, narrow eyes gleamed at her from the doorway. "Master says bring all you clean clothes an' shoes when you an' Dansaa bring horses. You tell that Walter, too."

"Clothes?" Jamesina asked blankly. "But why?"

"La illa!" Nyaama sniffed. "I do not try see inside that man head. It be stuffed with tobacco leaves."

"Ruth" and "Walter" could hardly believe their quirk of good fortune. Jamesina, it turned out, was to ride the filly to the courthouse, and Attercap to lead Midnight—to save him the work of carrying a rider—in case Chal had a chance to enter him in a race. Biggs, as foul-mouthed and foul-tempered as usual, was to drive the wagon. He had shaved for the occasion and, once the colonel appeared, spoke in a perfectly respectable fashion. Attercap was astonished to hear such courteous words come from a mouth usually full of curses and foul names.

Attercap, like Jamesina, brought his second pair of shoes and his few bits of clean clothing, but if they were supposed to change, they were given no time for it. The colonel and his sons mounted up and set off at once. Jamesina tossed her bundle into the wagon as she rode past it, so Attercap tipped his in, too.

* * *

Court Day was not at all what Jamesina expected. The redbrick courthouse, built with four short wings that gave it the shape of a stout cross, stood at a crossroads. Jamesina could barely see it even from horseback because of the rowdy, shifting crowd as more horsemen and coaches arrived.

There were no solemn lawyers in black, no town or Crown officials in their formal finery, and no ladies. Rough, bearded fellows in ill-fitting coats, or no coats at all, mingled with servants and slaves, pinched-looking poor farmers, stout, comfortable-looking ones, and planters looking or trying to look grand and prosperous. The crowd was thickest around the tavern—the "ordinary"—nearby. Peddlers sold their wares, crying, "Pipes, fine clay pipes!" or, "Fritters, fresh fried!" Some men, having made an early start on the day, were already drunk and quarrelsome. Even these raised unsteady hats and veered aside as the great gentlemen of the county paced past.

Jamesina, suddenly anxious, fingered the letters in her apron pocket. Where were the magistrates? The bailiffs? Surely not all of these people had business at court! She would never have a chance to be heard.

"Leave the wagon there, Biggs," Colonel Leslie ordered as Chal tied his mount to a tree and took Midnight from Attercap. "The boy and girl will stay with it. Mollison, you will endeavor to sell the filly. Biggs will come with me. Where is your wife, Biggs? She was to be here."

Biggs rocked up on tiptoe to peer over the crowd. "Just coming, sir," he said with a gap-toothed grin.

A moment later, Mrs. Biggs hove into sight, making her way through the crowd outside the ordinary like a large gunship under full sail. Her size was considerable, her skin unhealthily pale, her mouth a thin, pinched line, and she had a sullen, red-eyed glare not surprising in someone married to Biggs. She was carrying a bundle of harness and leading a second mule, a jenny, laden with bulging sacks.

"Good morning, sir," she mumbled, with a nervous duck of her head at Colonel Leslie's brief nod.

"*Hup* with you, then," Biggs said, giving her a boost onto the wagon's seat, but no greeting. "You bide there," he ordered as he tossed the harness and the sacks into the wagon. "Keep an eye on things while me and the colonel does a touch of business."

As the men moved away, Jamesina slipped to the back of the wagon to rescue her own bundle and to change her apron for the clean one. Attercap, at the front of the wagon, worked to keep Mrs. Biggs's red-rimmed gaze on himself. He checked the jack mule's harness, though he did not know one strap from another. He pitched pebbles at a fence post. He climbed the bare-branched red maple tree to which the mules were tied.

"Here, boy, you come down from there," Mrs. Biggs cried as he scuttled upward.

"I'm only trying to see. Why are there so many people?"

Mrs. Biggs gave a loud snort that made her and the wagon jiggle. "Why? Why, f'r the big men to be seen to be big, the little ones t' grind their teeth in envy, and every one of 'em with an eye to padding his own purse, that's why."

"Are those the magistrates there, coming out of the tavern?" he asked as the crowd shifted.

She craned to see. "Aye. They'll be going for their swearings-in." She yawned, closed her eyes, and settled down into herself on the wagon seat as if her bulk had no bones inside to hold her upright.

Jamesina tucked the letters into the pocket of the clean apron, pulled her thin shawl over her shoulders, and darted across the road. Slipping around a passing carriage, she trotted alongside it until she could hide in the bustle near the front porch of the courthouse. The loud voices around her fell silent at the bellow of a court official from the courthouse doorway.

"Oyez, Oyez, Oyez! Silence is commanded in the court while His Majesty's justices are sitting, 'pon pain of imprisonment. All manner of persons as have anything to do at court, draw near and give y'r attendance, and if anyone have any plaint or suit, let them come forth and be heard. God save the king!"

The doors opened, and the crowd surged in. It swept Jamesina with it, and cast her up on the shore of the inner doorway. She clutched the letters in her pocket, and craned to see, but could not. A young man who spied her trying to peer over the shoulders in front of her vanished for a moment along the crowded hallway, and came back with a stool from one of the jury rooms. Setting it against the wall, he gave her a hand up with a tipsy grin.

The three justices' seats stood on a raised platform at the far end of the room, with the royal emblem of the lion and unicorn on the wall above them. Portraits of King George, Queen Caroline, Prince George, and a gentleman who might be the governor of Virginia hung on either side. The jury box was empty, but the clerk and two other officers of the court sat to one side. On the public side of the railing of the bar, the benches in the court were crammed full, and men stood elbow to elbow around the walls. They all held their hats on their laps or tucked under their arms. As the Clerk of the Court stood and began to swear in the justices and officers one by one, Jamesina recognized Colonel Leslie's powdered wig at the end of the first row and, beside it, Biggs's mouse-brown hair tied back with a straggly bit of cord.

Many of the men in the front two rows held papers. Some clutched sheaves of them. So many papers! She would never get a chance to speak to the justices. Colonel Leslie would finish his business, and that would be that. Unless—unless Justice Moon stayed on for the afternoon's horse race. If he did, she might slip the letters to him. Or into his pocket, or—

She clutched the letters tight in both hands, took a deep breath, and tried hard to ignore the anxious flutter in her stomach.

Their swearing-in done with, the justices replaced their tricorne hats atop their white wigs, and took their seats. The first business was Colonel Leslie's. Jamesina listened in growing panic as the justices witnessed and notarized a five-year lease of thirty acres of land on the Pulvey River, and the gift of two bondservants, to Edward Biggs, in place of the goods and money due by custom of the country to newly freed servants. The change in ownership of the two servants, Ruth Grover, age fifteen, and Walter Hurt, age seventeen, was noted on the copies of their indentures and stamped with the seal of the court.

"No!" Jamesina cried before aloud she could stop herself. Not Mr. Biggs. Not now!

Curious heads turned. In panic, she slipped down from the stool and wriggled her way out through the door, to flee down the hall. Only one or two saw Mr. Mollison catch her by the arm and drag her out through the arcaded porch where servants and slaves waited, and hangers-on hung on.

Only the tipsy young man at the rear of the court-room saw the letters fall to the floor. He picked them up, and peered at what was written on one of them.

The Honorable Justice, Mr. Moon.

23

JAMESINA WOKE IN CONFUSION TO SEE BLURRED TREE-tops lurch past overhead, and lay among the bundles trying muzzily to make sense of it. Where was she? Where had she been? One eye felt swollen, and the cheekbone below it ached.

"Are ye all right?"

It was Attercap's whisper, but Jamie could not see him. She realized after a moment that she was in the farm cart, along with Mrs. Biggs's bundles and a clutch of hens crammed into a willow cage with a motheaten-looking rooster. She lifted a hand to touch her swollen eye, and the other hand came with it. Bewildered, Jamesina peered at the strip of rag that tied them together. Awkwardly, she struggled to sit up, only to be jounced down again as the cart jolted on its way.

"*Are* ye all right?"

Twisting around, Jamesina saw Attercap's hand on the rim of the cart, and him peering over it. He was trotting alongside. To his question, Jamesina nodded an uncertain "yes."

"What happened?" she mumbled.

"Ye don't remember?" He grinned a wide grin. "Och, 'twas a lovely brawl! Mr. Mollison hauled ye out from the court, and ye fought like a wild, mad ewe, butting and kicking and biting. But then the old cow took up an axe handle and gave ye a clout wi' it."

Up on the swaying driver's seat, Mrs. Biggs turned a squinty eye over her shoulder and called over the creak and rattle of harness and wagon and wheels. "I ain't deaf, boy. You shut your jabber," she snapped, and turned back to slap the reins on the two mules' rumps. Mr. Biggs was somewhere out of sight ahead.

Jamesina pulled herself up to cling to the side of the cart. "When?" she asked muzzily.

Attercap was jogging along beside her. "This morning. 'Tis midafternoon now."

Jamesina stared at him. He was still grinning, even though his lower cheek on one side was swollen, and the dried trace of a nosebleed smeared across it. He saw her stare and touched his fingertips to it, and winced a little.

"You're a rare sight yourself. A lovely black and purple," he said cheerfully, but then shivered. "The giff-gaff is, they will have us paying for it for a long while to come."

They journeyed another mile before Jamesina remembered the letters. She snatched at her apron pocket with her bound hands and, finding it empty, rooted in panic under the sacks as far as she could reach. They were not there. Keeping a watchful eye on Mrs. Biggs's back, she wriggled around to search the bed of the cart underneath her.

The letters were gone. Attercap had been watching, and he answered her silent question with a shake of his head. The letters had not fallen out during the struggle on the green, or when she was bundled into the cart.

In late afternoon, Mr. Biggs untied Jamesina's wrists, and ordered her down from the wagon to walk. The walking was much easier than the riding, for their way through the forest was a wagoner's nightmare. Only roughly cleared, and often muddy, it was crisscrossed by roots, and studded with stones and the stumps of fresh-cut trees. A few stumps had been hewn close to the ground, but many more had been cut with inches enough to lift a wheel up and drop it and the wagon down with a judder and thud. Biggs led the way, striding ahead of the mules, using his whip when they balked. The mules, lashed from before and behind by Biggses, labored on. The jack that old Baabukar had ridden struggled to pull his weight, but it was the jenny that pulled the heavy cart.

Before long a large stack of lumber—logs split into rails—came into view ahead. Biggs stopped Mrs. Biggs and the mules and strode back with a warning.

"We're on th' colonel's land agin. Up here aways, the track bends off toward the new fields his men are clearing. Just so none of yer old friends take it in their heads t' come snoopin' along after us, you two climb back in the cart and hunker down out o' sight. Where we're off to, we don't want callers. Did ye hear? Move! I can beat ye t' ribbons if I wish it, for I'm my own man, now. Ye hear? No more masters nor magistrates nor kings f'r me! Only King Biggs and the Biggses. Do as we please, and divil take th' rest of 'em. Right, old woman?"

"'Sright," his wife said, and, "gee-yup!" Jamesina and Attercap had to run to scramble into the moving cart.

The cart did not have far to go. The track was cleared

for only a few hundred yards further. Where it vanished, Biggs led the mules a short way through the close-crowding trees, and stopped where a rocky outcrop hunched up among them.

"Out ye get, ye two!" Biggs ordered. He began to unhitch the jenny mule, and Mrs. Biggs climbed awkwardly down from her perch. "This is far as the cart goes until we clear a way. Haul out the birds' cage and them bags."

"And set 'em somewheres dry," the woman snapped. She gave Jamesina a push, and Attercap a cuff on the ear, then shook out her shawl. Draping it over her head, she repinned its tails across her chest. The air was cold in the forest shade.

Attercap and Mr. Biggs ran the cart down a small slope and in under the broad ledge at the base of the rock. The opening there might have given shelter to a hunter or two, but was barely deep enough to cover the cart from the weather. Attercap and Jamesina were put to work gathering a great heap of dead brush and branches to hide it from chance passersby. The Biggses tied their sacks of belongings together and slung them over the mules' backs. Then, using a rock for a step up, they mounted, and set off. Jamesina and Attercap were left to struggle after them over the damp, slippery carpet of dead leaves. They carried a heavy sack apiece. The cage of chickens swayed between them.

At dusk, Biggs still pressed on, determined not to make camp for the night in the forest. Jamesina and Attercap fell further and further behind. A cold drizzle of rain began to fall, and they grew fearful that they would lose the trail in the dark. By the time Biggs's shout came and they saw the glimmer of a fire far ahead, they were almost too weary to be glad. When instead of a campfire they saw the square of a lighted window and the dark bulk of a cabin in the clearing ahead, they were much too weary for surprise.

Colonel Leslie, if he had bothered to think about anything but Shaws, would have wondered at Biggs's determination to move inland in the middle of winter. For a year, the Biggs's sons had worked at more than clearing the land promised to their father. With his help as often as he could steal away, they had built a cabin. Cabin, fences, woodpiles, mucky pigpen, all had a ramshackle, careless air—including the two younger Biggses and the sow and young pigs. The cabin itself had a shaggy, almost shapeless look. Its split-log siding still wore the rough bark, and the unfinished roof wore a makeshift thatch of bundled brush. Only the horses tied to a post by the cabin door looked trim and respectable.

Mrs. Biggs herded Jamesina and Attercap up a pole ladder to the cabin's loft after a skimpy supper of cold corn bread. They were left to shiver under a thin coverlet on a floor made of cane poles. "There's no shutters on that window up there," Biggs said. "It's good as a door. Better tie them two up, boys, for fear they slip out on us. And their hands *behind* 'em, you knotheads, or they'll loose each other afore you're down the ladder."

When they did come down the ladder, they removed it.

"Good thinking," Biggs said. "Now mebbe you'll tell me where them two horses out there come from."

"Found 'em in the woods," the older young man said. "Honest we did. 'Twas two days ago. We went off to trap beaver in the foothills, and strayed higher'n we meant to—and there they was! We reckoned they was wild, and ours."

"Hah!" Biggs crowed with pleasure. Once supper

was on the table, he raised a cup of ale. "Here's t' the year's free rent the colonel don't know we've had, and this year's crop t'come. Them two in the loft don't look like there's much work in 'em, but we'll squeeze it all out."

When at last the fire died down on the hearth, the four Biggses spread out their bedding, and slept.

At dawn, Jamesina and Attercap woke to a shrill, warbling yell, and the air full of terrible cries.

24

INDIANS.

The sounds of gunshots, screams, and struggle were mingled with wild, terrifying cries that were meant, like the screams of panthers, to strike terror into their prey. Jamesina, lying bound on the floor of the loft, felt strangely calm. To her ears, the shrill yells seemed much like she imagined the wild cries of Highland clansmen would be as they fell upon a camp of cattle lifters. It was a world she understood. But then, Attercap might say, she would. To many Scots as well as to the English, Highlanders were wild men. Hadn't England's King George said when he sent his Highland troops to America, that he was "sending savages to fight savages"?

She had known the horses meant trouble. She had seen that they were not wild, or newly tamed. They stood at ease at their hitching post. Runaways, or stolen from some upland settler, she had thought. She had not thought of Indians. Indian country lay beyond the mountains, people said. Perhaps so, but she guessed that these had come for their horses. And to punish the thieves.

Gunfire came from all sides, from the roughly cleared field as well as the forest. In her mind, Jamesina could see the shapes of men crouched in the long morning shadows behind the great tree stumps. Attercap was terrified. He squirmed around so that he lay on his other side, facing Jamesina.

"No! Do not stir," she whispered fiercely.

He moved his head in a shadow of a nod, and clenched his eyes shut.

Before long, the ragged gunfire from below died out. The only cries were whoops of triumph, and those soon gave way to the sounds of rummaging and loud voices beneath the loft. Their speech was as strange to Jamesina as her own Gaelic had been to the Aberdeenshire boys.

"To titsatu ka!"

"Tsulasgi—skhvhsi!"

"Selu—witsiko wthiha!" Wood splintered, and the hens set up a great squawking.

The voices moved back out of doors. Soon the smell of smoke drifted through the loft window, and then the aroma of roasting chicken. At that, Attercap's eyes opened, and he raised his eyebrows hopefully at Jamesina, as if to ask, *They'll go when they've eaten, won't they?* When he saw she had no answer, he shut his eyes again.

At the sudden sound of a horse nickering, and of hooves trampling, Jamesina began to wonder. Perhaps they were moving off. Perhaps Attercap was right to hope. Perhaps. She did not move.

An answer was not long in coming. A blazing stick snatched from the chickens' cookfire arched up past the window, aimed to light on the end of the brushwood roof. The thatch overhead blazed up with a swift flash and crackle and roar.

"Mo creach! Cuidich sinn!" Jamesina shouted. She rocked up onto her knees to scramble toward the edge of the loft, and Attercap struggled awkwardly to his feet. "Help!" he bellowed.

Ash and blazing twigs blew toward them, and he dropped back to the cane floor.

Excited voices shouted outside.

"Ayotli! Galuhlatitli!"

"Hihiyuha-ka!"

Suddenly the top of the ladder appeared at the loft's rim, then a hand clutching a war axe. A fierce, dark-eyed face rose above it, with long hair flowing loose like shimmering black water. The dark eyes belonged to a young woman. They widened in surprise—and then widened further. Two frightened young whites? With their hands bound behind them? She hesitated for only a moment, and then was up and kneeling between them, thrusting her axe into her belt, drawing a knife to cut their bonds, and motioning them to follow.

Before they reached the foot of the ladder, the entire roof was ablaze. Embers fell like red snow, and the cabin was filled with smoke as they stumbled toward the door.

Outside, a dozen barefoot, shaven-headed warriors watched the three emerge, red-eyed and coughing, into the cold morning sunshine, and raised their rifles.

One moved forward. *"Halewis-da!"*

Neither Jamesina nor Attercap had ever seen what the Virginians called a "wild Indian"—or a tame one—though they had heard that there were Indian slaves on a plantation not far from Shaws. They turned uncertainly to the woman. Her face told them nothing, but she pointed to the raw marks where the ropes had chafed Jamesina's wrists.

"*Atsinatla'i utowela,*" she said to the men, and the anger faded a little from their painted faces. Turning, she asked sharply in English, "Bond slaves?"

Startled, Jamesina and Attercap only nodded.

With a faint glimmer of humor at their startled looks, the young woman said, "How do you say? Out of fire and into cook pan?"

They were Cherokees, mountain people. The young woman's name was Nanyehi. She was beautiful in a strong-faced way, and her hair hung down to the backs of her knees.

"I learn English from my father," she said as she gave them what was left of the last roast chicken, and a little parched corn. "He was Lenapé. He live among English before they drive Lenapé from Lenapé country."

Nanyehi was with the raiders because she refused to be parted from her husband. "If Tsulu hunts, I hunt. If he goes with warriors to make war, I go." She traveled with him on every hunt, and now, in time of war, fought at his side.

Jamesina and Attercap exchanged a quick, startled look.

"War?" they asked.

"You do not know this?" Nanyehi asked. "English begin this war. They kill fourteen warriors and steal horses. Always the English governors promise no English come west from the lowlands, but they do not keep this promise." With a sweep of her arm, she took in the blazing cabin where the Biggses had fallen, the woodpile now a bonfire, and the dead mule—old Baabukar's mule, that could not pull its weight. "Like these people steal two of our horses that break their—their hobble," she said calmly. "So the Cherokee bring war here."

She turned to explain to the tall man at her side what she had told the two white slaves. The man wore a butternut-colored European shirt over his leggings, and a leather belt with a decorated pouch hanging from it. His head was shaved, like the others', of all but a roach of hair that, stiffened with red-deer hair, stood up in a ridge from front to back along the top of his head. Like the others', his face and neck and arms were tattooed with curious patterns of lines, some wavy, some jagged. His cheeks were painted with black crosses.

He turned to the men with him and spoke quietly. They nodded in agreement, then moved quickly. One vanished with his rifle into the forest. Others brought the horses that had come with them, the two recovered ones and the young mule. They filled the Biggses' sacks with what they had taken from the house. Tying them together, they slung them and their own packs across the animals' withers. One brought the haunches of the slaughtered pig to add to a sack, and two others came carrying a squealing piglet in each hand by a hind leg. Sitting on their heels, they took leather thongs and bound the piglets' feet together.

No one seemed to be in command. When a laughing argument arose—about who would walk and who would ride, since they had only the six mounts—it was settled by chance. One man took from his pouch a handful of beans blackened on one side, and they sat on their heels to take turns throwing the beans to the ground. The winners, the six who had more beans fall with the light side up, went to seize the rope halters of their mounts. Leaping onto their backs, they rode around the burning cabin with shrill whoops, two waving their rifles, and one swinging the Biggses' black iron stewpot. And then they vanished into the forest.

As the walls of the fiery cabin fell inward, Jamesina felt sick. The Biggses had been cruel and mean-minded, but they had cared for each other. It was not right that they should die for being too stupid or too greedy to see that a horse was not wild. Jamesina knew that horse thieves or cattle lifters in her own Highlands might come to the same harsh end, but that was no comfort.

The young woman Nanyehi prodded Jamesina with her rifle barrel. "You come. You, girl, and boy-like-a-stick, you carry pigs."

Attercap swallowed. "Ye've set us free. Can ye not let us go?"

The look she gave him was impassive, but it seemed for a moment as if she were considering it. Then she shrugged. "You are not free. You are slaves. We take you with us to the River Tanasi, to Slave Catcher. When this war is finish, perhap he sell you to English."

Cherokee Country

1760

25

THE JOURNEY THROUGH THE FOOTHILLS AND INTO THE mountains was slow, and through dense forest all the way. The higher they climbed, the sharper the cold grew. The Cherokees pulled moccasins and deerskin mantles from their packs and donned them.

March became April. It was too late for snow, even in the mountains, but in the mornings a crisp hoarfrost shimmered on the trees and ground as white as snowfall. Frost crusted the trees and crunched underfoot until a midmorning sun burned it away.

Jamesina was not much bothered by the cold or by sleeping on the ground, but Attercap felt them bitterly. "'Twas good fortune we slept that night in Biggs's loft with our shoes on," he said with grim cheer. "But we should have saved the coverlet." Because they were made to tend the fire, taking turns to sleep and feed it, it hardly mattered that at nightfall they had only one skin blanket between them. At first they were watched carefully, but after the fourth day were left to bring up the rear. They had come so far into the wilderness that there was little chance that they could find their way back to Virginia. The Cherokees knew they had no choice but to struggle on.

The struggle was made much harder by the young pigs. Jamesina and Attercap carried them tucked up one under each arm. They could feed them on parched corn, or morel mushrooms or edible roots when these could be found. Still, the piglets seemed to grow heavier each day, their struggles stronger, and their squeals louder.

When the last of the pork from the sow was roasted and eaten, the Indians had no need to slaughter the piglets. They killed a bear and dined on rich bear meat for three days. On the only day after that when the hunters came across no turkeys or deer, they brought out dried venison to eat with bear's oil for sauce. For their captives, having full stomachs was such a pleasure after a year of never enough, that the hardships hardly mattered.

Twice, the party sheltered for the night in the mouths of caves where their firelight glittered on stalactites and stalagmites deeper in the caverns. Once, they heard the scream of a panther from deep in the cave, but either because of the fire, or because they were too many, it did not show itself. Most nights, the Cherokees sat up late around the fire, to sing songs and tell tales. Their laughter and wonder at the tales were a torment to Attercap, who loved stories and hated not understanding theirs. He began to ask Nanyehi questions about the old legends and adventures, and about what this word meant, and that.

On one such night by the fire, they talked of the war. Tsulu spoke in Cherokee, and then Nanyehi in English, with great bitterness. "We try to make peace. We even give your king land for two forts in our country. After

Virginians kill our men, we raid those who take our land. The Beloved Warrior Aganstata and other great men go with white flag to Charleston to seek peace, to say, 'All is now even.' But Guv'nor Litta-ton he will not make peace. And he has no honor. He orders soldiers to lock up our great men in Fort Prince George."

"For hostages?" Attercap asked sharply.

"To trade for warriors who kill the land stealers, he *say*. . . ."

"But if they went with a flag of truce, that is treachery!" Jamesina exclaimed.

Nanyehi nodded. "When Aganstata and warriors try to rescue them, to make all even again, soldiers kill all those great men, from all our towns. *That* is why we make war."

The spirits of the warriors rose day by day as they traveled south. Jamesina and Attercap decided it must mean they were near the end of their journey. One night they laughed and were very merry after they ate. The next afternoon they crossed a swift, cold creek, and three or four miles further on reached the bank of a broad river Nanyehi called the Tanasi. On the far side, smoke rose like threads from at least a hundred fires. Not far downstream, other, smaller clusters of smoke arose.

"You see!" Nanyehi cried proudly. "Itsati, chief town of the Overhill Cherokees."

Tsulu and the other warriors raised their rifles with shrill cries and fired into the air. Moments later, canoes appeared upon the river, and soon Jamesina and Attercap found themselves bundled in with the pigs and the baggage, racing across the water.

Whatever they expected, it was not the town they saw. Awestruck, they stared at more than a hundred thatched houses scattered across the wide river meadow. Southeast of the town, a great, fenced-in field and paddock held hundreds of horses. Orchards of winter-naked fruit trees dotted the outskirts of the settlement. Beyond these, lines of narrow fields stretched away to the south and west. Most astonishing of all, at the end of a wide way leading up from the riverside, a huge, windowless structure bulked up in the middle of the town like a small mountain.

On the bank a noisy crowd, mostly children and women, with some older men and women, was gathered to welcome the warriors. They stared with open curiosity at the two young strangers who stepped out of a canoe. Jamesina and Attercap stared back with equal curiosity, but warily, and wondered what Nanyehi and Tsulu and their companions were telling the others about their captives. The faces were not unfriendly. Jamesina was more fascinated than frightened, but she could not forget the tales the servants at Shaws told of the dreadful cruelties Cherokees were said to practise on their prisoners. Things much worse than what had happened to the Biggses . . .

As the crowd scattered, Nanyehi pointed to the pigs, squirming on their sides in the bottom of the nearest canoe. "Bring them," she commanded, and set off after her husband.

Jamesina and Attercap followed quickly, with the pigs. They were so absorbed in all they saw that even Attercap's habit of caution was overcome by curiosity. He gaped, and poured out a flood of questions, and shook his head in wonder. The houses, most of them windowless, were built of frameworks of poles woven together with vines and branches, and covered with a smooth plaster of pale mud. Jamesina marveled at the thatched pitched roofs with smoke holes at the top. The same roofs topped old stone houses in Gairloch. But the great mountain of a building at the head of the wide path up from the river—if it was a building and not a mound—was truly strange. Framed by a tree-trunk pillar on each side and another across the top as lintel, its narrow doorway was dwarfed by the great, grassy, seven-sided shape that rose above it.

Attercap gazed up at the mound building in amazement, and craned to look back over his shoulder as they moved away among the houses. Jamesina, thinking of the sod houses she had been in at home in Scotland, with their thick walls and small rooms, looked back, too, in wonder that such a great weight of wall could stand at all.

Nanyehi led them to the outskirts of the town, and a pen where a stout sow lifted up her head and snuffled with interest at their approach.

"Her name is Kama'ma—'Butterfly.' She has no litter," Nanyehi explained as the sow trotted toward them, "and so she steals young ones from the others. She can look after these." She took her knife from its sheath at her belt and cut the cords that bound their trotters. The four piglets fell, stood up, and staggered toward Kama'ma.

"Leave them, and come," Nanyehi ordered. "We must eat before dark, for then I go with Tsulu to council. You will grind corn and tend our fire, then sleep. Tomorrow you work."

The young pigs' eager squeals were fading behind them as they passed a thatch-roofed shelter with unplastered walls only partly covered with deerhide. Two gaunt, ragged women stood silently in the doorway. Five others and several children huddled over a small fire outside and watched in silence as the three passed. They all appeared to be English.

"Who are those women?" Jamesina asked when they reached Nanyehi's house.

"Are they slaves, too?" Attercap asked.

"No. Prisoners," Nanyehi answered. "Taken in raids. But safe here. Itsati is 'Beloved Town' of the Cherokee. Blood cannot to be spilled in Itsati." She cocked her head. "Do I speak right?"

"'May not be,'" Jamesina said with a blink of surprise. "Or 'Must not be spilled.'"

"Not *any*one's?" Attercap asked in unbelief.

Nanyehi nodded. "It is true. Even killer is safe here from revenge. But you do not stay. One day soon I take you to Taskigi, to the house of Atagulkalu, my uncle, who is head man there. He will take you over the river to Slave Catcher's camp."

Nanyehi's house was simply furnished, with low beds covered with furs, and shelves along the walls to hold storage baskets. And indeed it was Nanyehi's house, not Tsulu's. As she explained to her new slaves, in Cherokee country all of the houses and gardens and fields belonged to the women.

"Not like English," she said. "Here, girl, here is corn to grind. You, boy, bring wood from outside and I build fire."

Just before nightfall, Nanyehi and Tsulu and all the other men and women of the town went out from their houses onto the dusk-filled paths to make their way to the council. Jamesina and Attercap took the buffalo skins they had been given, spread them out on the smooth floor mats of split cane, close to the fire, and slept.

Warm and comfortable for the first time in more than a year, Jamesina dreamed that she was in her own bed at Grudidh House, listening to a faint, distant skirl of bagpipes float down across the waters of Loch Maree from Letterewe, three miles away.

26

"BAGPIPES?" ATTERCAP ASKED IN SURPRISE.

He and Jamesina grasped the pole on which the full skin water bag hung, and struggled to lift it free of the river. It swayed between them as they staggered up the pathway. Once they had it balanced, Attercap looked at Jamesina curiously.

"Why are you weeping?"

"I'm *not,*" she said quickly, shaking her head so that her hair swung forward and he could not see. "Why would I weep over a dream?"

"Dream?" Attercap stopped suddenly, and the water bag swung heavily on its pole. "But it was no dream. I heard it."

"You *heard* it?" Jamesina turned to stare at him. "What do you mean?" she whispered. "Why didn't you tell me?"

"I thought it a half-dream," he explained as they moved on. "But now—do you remember that Nanyehi once spoke of two English forts in Cherokee country? One must be—"

"Close by," Jamesina finished eagerly. "And with Highland troops. Highlanders! But where? Oh! The English prisoners will know. They must know. I can talk to them—I'll go at once. As soon as we've filled the water pots." Her eyes shone.

"No," Attercap cautioned. "Wait for the chance to come by itself. 'Tis a pity, for I like them, but these Cherokee folk are enemies. Even Nanyehi. We are watched. Be sure of it."

Attercap was next sent to work in the horse paddock and fields. Jamesina—trembling with impatience—was put to work with the English prisoners in the household gardens south of Itsati. The fields were long, narrow strips like the rigs on Jamesina's grandfather's farm, winter-dressed with wood ashes and horse dung. The women dug the moist earth with strong digging sticks, turning under the ash and manure. Planting time would come soon.

The work was not easy, but the Cherokee women and girls worked hard beside them, each woman on her own long strip of ground, each with her girl children, or slave, or a prisoner. To Jamesina's dismay, every time she looked up, the English women in the fields on either side of Nanyehi's were always digging at the furthest end from the spot where she was at work.

In late morning, Nanyehi went away and returned with water, and meat and corn cakes on a basketwork tray to share with her new slave. But no one fed the prisoners. They sat in two or three little groups and shared a few scraps pulled from their own pockets. Afterward, Jamesina watched more openly as she worked. She saw that when the work was finished on one strip the English women were pushed to another where there still was more to do. If they worked too slowly, the owners of the fields pushed or struck them with the digging sticks. Yet though Nanyehi shoved Jamesina and spoke sharply a time or two, no one else had touched her.

"'Tis because we belong to no one," muttered the stringy blond girl Jamesina finally caught up to. "If they touched you 'twould be an insult to Nanyehi the War Woman. They only keep us until they can ask for ransom."

Jamesina bent over her digging stick. "The English fort—where is it?" she asked in a low voice. "We heard the bagpipes. Is it near?"

"Fort Loudon? Oh, 'tis near enough. Not far past Taskigi," the girl muttered. She loosened and broke up another clod of earth. "But it might as well be far as the moon. They always watch. And the fort is surrounded." She darted a look toward Nanyehi, who was digging her way toward them, and moved away quickly.

Taskigi. Taskigi, where Nanyehi's uncle lived. Where she and Attercap were to be taken. What could be better?

But weeks passed, and the trip to Taskigi did not happen.

Each day after midday Nanyehi left Jamesina to work on her own. Attercap, who had only once in his life been on a horse, was delighted to be learning to ride as well as to care for the horses. Jamesina was impatient to be moving on. Her longing for each day to be over and tomorrow to come made the long rows, the digging, and the planting seem endless. Then one day at midafternoon Nanyehi came to call her back to the house. She gave her a push toward the path. "You will grind corn and crack nuts. I cook. Tonight is a great feast."

With the food prepared and cooking in clay pots and

the Biggses' iron stew kettle, Nanyehi changed her shirt and leggings for a cloth skirt and embroidered wrist-length cape. Next, she fastened back and folded up her hair and tied it into a heavy club shape on her neck with a leather cord and bright red ribbon. Then she went to sit cross-legged in the doorway with Tsulu to paint his face and decorate his roach with fresh red-dyed deer's hair, and beads and feathers.

After a look or two over her shoulder in their direction, Nanyehi frowned and tossed her carved, wooden comb to Jamesina. "You both," she ordered. At something Tsulu said, she rose and rooted through a storage basket to bring out two pairs of deerskin moccasins. She threw them at Attercap's feet. "For both. Your shoes all holes."

Attercap hastily rubbed at his dirty feet. When he began to pull on the moccasins at once, horse-dung smell or no, Nanyehi frowned and sent him out to wash his feet in the river.

Jamesina struggled to pull the comb through the dark red tangled curls that had not been unsnarled since the day she left Shaws. She watched as Nanyehi crouched down to remove the cooking pots from the coals and push the baking stone aside, then brought gourds holding water and sand to put out the fire. Jamesina was puzzled. The corn cakes on the stone might have baked through, but the chunks of meat in the stew were far from tender. And the Cherokees over-cooked everything.

Nanyehi saw her puzzlement. "Tonight we put out all fires," she explained. "All fires in Itsati. Tonight is *Atsila danalisda' yuhusguh*. The Feast of New Fire."

For a moment Jamesina did not move. "My people have such a feast, too," she said slowly.

Nanyehi gave Jamesina a startled look—and then a considering one. "I think maybe you come. Why not?"

Before dusk, at the sound of singing and drums and rattles, the women and men of Itsati left their houses. On the wide path that circled the council house, they were met by dancers painted all over in white with whorls and crosses of red. One more frightening than the rest, painted all in red with a white stripe down each arm and leg, shook gourd rattles as he danced. By leaps and drumbeat, they led the way to the dark door in the council house, and vanished through it when their dance was finished. The doorway was so narrow that only one person could enter at a time, and the interior was dark and full of murmurs.

Nanyehi led Jamesina by the hand. Attercap kept close at her heels. Once inside, they followed blindly along a winding way and up steps, until Nanyehi stopped and pushed Jamesina down onto a seat.

Her eyes adjusted slowly to the faint light that fell from the smoke hole far above. She found herself in a great, high hall where hundreds of men and women sat on benches rising in rows around the seven walls. So many! There were places for perhaps five hundred, though many—those of warriors out on raids—remained empty. Jamesina looked around her. Tsulu was nowhere to be seen.

"He sits with the *Anikawi,* his mother's clan, on the far side," Nanyehi said. "Here we are my mother's people, the *Aniwaya.* The seven sides of the house are for the seven clans." She pointed to shadowy men and women on the half-empty front benches, where tobacco pipes passed from hand to hand. "They are head man

Kanagatuckco and our Beloveds, great in war. The gray-hair woman is the Karanu Waninahi. She is War Woman and great one from Nikwasi."

The great hall fell silent as a tall man rose from the front bench, and moved out onto the floor's wide circle. He began to speak in phrases so musical that Jamesina wondered if it were a song, and his gestures pointed again and again to the circle of stones at the floor's center. There was no fire in the circle, only three tall poles of cane placed upright in the earth and a narrow band of tinder that spiraled inward toward the center. The man's speech was long. When he finished, the red-painted man entered the circle. Out of doors, dusk had deepened into evening. In the darkness of the council house nothing now could be seen but the red man's white stripes, and the three pale poles. Like a white stick figure the man danced and sang around the circle, and struck the top of one tall cane and then the next with a club. By inches, he drove the canes into the ground. When nothing more could be seen of them, the dancer held up his white stick arms and moved back. The drums fell silent. The hall grew still.

Jamesina's heart raced even though she did not know what was about to happen. The excitement—and fear—in the dark hall was like a great, shared heartbeat.

And then one thin, pale thread of smoke rose from one of the canes buried in the fire circle.

A great, soft sigh filled the hall.

A moment later a soft, glowing light appeared. It was perhaps the size of a small walnut. A deep murmur arose as the glow moved into the tinder and on toward the center of the circle in a slow, narrowing spiral. There, it flared into flame and the hall was filled with a shout of triumph. Fire tenders ran forward with bundles of cane splints to feed the fire.

Jamesina breathed out slowly. *"How?"* she whispered.

"I do not know," Nanyehi said. "The fire comes up from the earth to light the tinder. It is great medicine. Great magic. Now the fires all will be lighted and there will be eating and dancing. After Beginning Dance and Friendship Dance come dances to pray friendship and good health of birds and animals we need."

As the council fire grew, the vast hall brightened until light touched the wooden ribs and close-woven framework arching high overhead. Jamesina saw little of it. She was remembering how in her other world she had danced around the need-fire bonfire. *And Grandfather blessed the animals. And all the fires were lit again.* . . . It was a mystery and wonder to her that two worlds parted by so wide a sea could echo each other so nearly—and yet be so unlike.

Women moved down to the fire circle. Each in turn lighted a long wand of cane to take home to her fire. Jamesina and Attercap followed Nanyehi down, aware all the way of curious black eyes. By the front benches, the gray-haired woman—whose title, Karanu, Nanyehi explained, meant Raven, or war leader—rose to walk with Nanyehi. Her face was barely middle-aged, much younger-looking than the gray hair had suggested. She gave Jamesina and Attercap only a fleeting glance, but all the while she spoke with Nanyehi, her eyes moved restlessly over the line of fireseekers and up and along the rows of benches, where the men still sat. The only word of their talk that Jamesina could make out was Atagulkalu, the name of Nanyehi's uncle. The Raven spoke his name several times. Once, Nanyehi shot a quick glance behind her, as if to be sure that Jamesina and Attercap had stayed close.

Suddenly, the Raven gave Jamesina a sharp look up and down, and shot a question at her in English. "Do you know write English, girl?"

Startled, Jamesina nodded.

"Good. I take her. I take them," the Raven said to Nanyehi. They spoke together in Cherokee for a moment, and then the Raven turned again to Jamesina. "You and boy. Tomorrow we go Nikwasi."

27

JAMESINA AND ATTERCAP ROSE BEFORE DAWN THE NEXT morning, but the Raven and six other warriors from Nikwasi were at the horse paddock before them.

"These for you." The gray-haired woman warrior nodded toward the two horses standing beside her own. Each had a pair of knotted net sacks, both empty, slung across its withers. One was a young gelding with a lively eye, the other a placid, broad-backed mare.

"*Asehi,* I see that she is for me," Attercap said with a quick grin. "Tsulu has told you that even I can keep my seat on a bench that wide."

Either the Raven Waninahi did not understand all of the English words, or she thought the joke too small to earn a smile. "We go," she said. Grasping her horse's mane, she leaped astride and with a kick set him off at a trot with the others close beside or behind. Jamesina managed to mount the same way, but awkwardly. Attercap, not in the least embarrassed, pulled the mare close to the rock the small children used for mounting, clambered aboard, and followed.

From the horse fields, the path ran eastward away from Itsati and into the forest. In less than a mile they came out onto cleared land, and saw ahead the orchards, fields, and houses and council house of another town, not much smaller than Itsati. "Sitiku," said one of the warriors, naming it as he pointed. Half a dozen young children out hunting birds with blowguns made from cane stalks stopped at the sight of the riders, and ran after them into the town. Older boys and girls were playing at a game in which a bowler bowled a polished stone, and the others threw long lances to see who could come nearest, but they stopped their game and followed, too. The path passed among the spread-out houses toward the southern edge of Sitiku, and everywhere people came out to greet the Raven, or ask for news, or to press food upon the travelers.

For each wrapped cake or pouch of parched corn that went into his net sacks, Attercap bowed from his perch and said, *"Wuh-don!"* At each *"Wuh-don!"* the grins of the Nikwasi warriors grew wider until at last they burst into laughter.

Attercap was puzzled. "What is it? Does it no' mean 'thank you'?"

The Raven's grin was as wide as any. "Yes. Almost. But your ear is more thick yet than English ears. It is *'Wadan'—'Wah-dahn.'"* As she spoke the word, she made Attercap's *d* almost a *t*, and the end of the word more nasal.

By the time they reached and forded the wide creek at the far side of the town, both Jamesina's and Attercap's sacks were half full. It was much the same a mile and a half further on, in a tiny town halfway to Talasi. There, the people brought water gourds and a sweet bread made from corn and chestnut flours. Attercap remembered its name at his first bite. *"Diskwah-ni! Wah-dah-nyuh!"* He shrugged cheerfully as the grins reappeared. Though the warriors laughed at his attempts, they were pleased, too, and corrected him. One or two who spoke a little English tried to answer his eager questions about the names of animals and plants and trees they saw, and about their families.

Near Talasi itself, the hills crowded closer to the wide River Tanasi, and their path through the forest turned south away from the river and climbed beside a creek into the hills. In a few miles they were in the mountains, climbing toward a narrow pass. When the slopes grew so steep that the horses began to labor, the warriors dismounted. Jamesina, not much used to riding without a saddle, and Attercap, who had ridden only in the horse fields, had struggled to keep from slipping off backwards, and were thankful to reach the ground at last. To their surprise, instead of leading the horses upward, the Cherokees removed their bridles and sent them off downhill with a slap to the shoulder or rump. Jamesina and Attercap exchanged a look as they did the same—this, perhaps, was how the Biggs boys came to find their new horses.

The warriors coiled up their bridles, packed them into their deerskin shoulder bags, and climbed on. Jamesina and Attercap bundled theirs into the food sacks, and followed.

At the head of the pass, the travelers climbed above the path to sit among the firs and look out over the tree-clad mountains heaped up in rumpled ridges from the bright green at their feet to a pale gray-blue at the sky's far edge. *"Shacona-ge,"* the Raven said, sweeping an arm from northeast to southwest. "Place of blue smoke."

"Why," Attercap asked suddenly, "do you need someone to write English?"

The Raven answered slowly, feeling for the right English words. "We see English people talk much with paper. Not face-to-face. If Guvnor in Charles Town will not hear Aganstata and Atagulkalu when they speak peace face-to-face, we will write to him their words. We will make him know he cannot bind all Cherokees to a word spoken by one, or to words on paper only one puts his mark on."

"But if the one is a chief—" Jamesina began.

The Raven's black eyes snapped with impatience. "'Chief'! 'King'! White-man words. Our great men do not rule. If a great man speaks peace in council, wise heads say, 'Make it so,' and they keep at home. But young men hot for war, they do not listen. No Cherokee rules another. English do not understand this. This girl will write it."

"But why me?" Jamesina asked. "Why not one of the English women in Itsati?"

The Raven shrugged. "English now are enemies. Nanyehi say you not English. She tell me trust you."

That, Jamesina thought, was odder still.

They were still sitting, eating a handful or two of parched corn, when twelve silent figures appeared on the path below. They carried not only rifles, but also bows and deerskin quivers full of arrows. The Raven raised a hand to her mouth and gave a sharp turkey call that stopped the newcomers in midstride. They were Nanyehi, Tsulu, one of the men who had been with them in Virginia, and one man each from nine of the other Overhill towns. They had come to gather news from the Valley and Middle and Lower towns and carry it home again. The Raven had been waiting for them.

Together, they traveled down through dark, still hemlocks and spruce fir into a land of spring-green forest, of rich thickets of flame-colored azaleas and bright mountain laurel, and of waterfalls, black bears, and red wolves, of steep trails, and deep, cold ravines.

The Raven Waninahi and the travelers from the Overhill towns came to Tsiyahi, the nearest of the Middle towns, at the hour of the evening meal. Attercap and Jamesina straggled in last, thankful that Nanyehi had slowed her own pace to keep them in sight so that they did not mistake the trail.

Skiagusta, the great man of the town, and his wife invited them into their house to share their roast venison, and a thick stew of corn and beans and pork.

The house was crowded, and smoky, for too little of the smoke from the fire found its way out through the hole in the roof. The smells and bare arms and tattoos were different, and they sat on the earthen floor instead of on low chairs, but the firelight, the reek of smoke, and the laughter made Jamesina's eyes sting with tears of homesickness. It might have been a gathering for a *ceilidh* in one of the smoky houses in the clachans above Grudidh House or Amgaldale. And yet . . . and yet, oddly, her bitter disappointment at the lost chance to reach the safety of the fort so near Itsati had vanished. That would have been a first step on the journey home, and yet she had an odd conviction—one that made no sense—that they had escaped some great danger. That—

A sudden dim halloo cut through the cheerful talk and laughter.

Every Cherokee in the room stiffened and fell silent at the drawn-out cry. In a few moments the room had emptied, and Jamesina and Attercap followed. Once through the doorway, they saw the people of Tsiyahi hurrying from their scattered houses toward the mound on which the council house stood. The cries that called them had come from a man perched at the peak of the high council-house roof. He gave one last shout through cupped hands, and was gone.

"It is the News call," Nanyehi said over her shoulder to Attercap's breathless question as they reached the council-house door. A moment later, just inside the door, two warriors barred their way and Skiagusta came out again to speak with Nanyehi.

"It is bad. You cannot come," she said quickly when he was gone. "You go, wait at Skiagusta house."

They were watching from the doorway of the head man's house when, only minutes later, the ten men from the Overhill towns who had traveled south with Nanyehi and Tsulu hurried from the council house to race north by the way they had come.

Dusk had only begun to gather when the Raven and her own companions, and Nanyehi and Tsulu themselves, reappeared.

"We go," the Raven ordered.

The news was frightening. A rider from the south had reached Itseyi, the southernmost of the Middle towns, with word that a great British army had marched into the Cherokee country and struck at Kuwahi in the night. Every man was killed, but the women and children had fled through the neighboring towns and warned them, so that many escaped into the hills. But every one of the Lower towns was burned, its cornfields trampled, its orchards cut down and pitched into the flames. The army now was camped at Fort Prince George, near the ruined towns. Its commander had sent messengers to Itseyi and Nikwasi and Watagi, and demanded the surrender of all Cherokee towns in exchange for peace.

The Raven Waninahi and her companions were desperate to reach Nikwasi. They set off at once to go as far as they could before dark. Tsulu would have given Jamesina and Attercap to Skiagusta and hurried on with them, but Nanyehi strangely, stubbornly, refused to leave her slaves. Jamesina and Attercap abandoned their moccasins to go barefoot and found their footing surer. Even so, before nightfall, they—and Nanyehi, who hung back to keep in sight of them—covered only half the ground that the Raven and the others did. They came behind them on the next day to the town of Tamatli. A rough track beyond Tamatli led to Watogi and to the Raven's Nikwasi, and other river towns, and on it they met messengers hurrying to the Valley towns in the west. There were women and children, too, in flight from the ruined Lower towns. On the following day, in Nikwasi itself, they saw many more.

Two days later, these were gone, sent northwest into the hills or to the further river towns. Nikwasi filled up with warriors—its own, hundreds from the other Middle towns, and in the next day and a half the first of hundreds more from the Valley and Overhill towns. All the while, Jamesina and Attercap wondered why they themselves were there.

And then, soon after the hour of sunrise, scouts brought word that the soldiers—redcoats in skirts, and bluecoats, and brownshirts—had marched out of Fort Prince George, on their way to Itseyi and Nikwasi.

Redcoats in skirts . . .

28

"WHY DID YOU BRING THEM HERE FROM TAMALI?" THE Raven had demanded of Nanyehi and Tsulu as the warriors gathered. There would be no writing letters of peace to the English now.

Nanyehi had left Jamesina and Attercap in Waninahi's daughter's house and warned them not to go out-of-doors on their own. There was great danger that in their fury at the destruction of the Lower towns, warriors who were strangers to them might strike out in grief and vengeance, taking them for English. She and Tsulu returned within the hour, carrying two plain deerskin belts and pouches, two short lengths of cane stoppered at each end, corn cakes for their slaves' morning meal, and news.

"Waninahi was not angry," Nanyehi added quickly. "She has no time for small things. All is hurry now."

"Why *did* you bring us?" Jamesina asked. She and Attercap had puzzled at that over the last days. Several times on their long journey down through the Middle towns Jamesina had sensed an odd intentness in Nanyehi, too faint to call a purpose. Almost a—listening. A waiting.

Tsulu, in the doorway, shrugged as he thrust his tomahawk into his belt and took up his weapons. "*I* not know," he growled, startling them with the English words as he vanished.

"I say to Waninahi that all then was hurry, too," was Nanyehi's answer to Jamesina's question. She rose. "I say I did not think. I only come."

Attercap moved to the door to peer out, for the shouts and bustle and drums had fallen quiet, and there was only the sound of passing feet. "What is happening?" he asked anxiously.

Outside, the town was already half emptied. Armed men moved past in war parties of thirty or forty, stripped to the waist and painted with the black slashes and designs of death and the red of success. The leader of each party or his attendant carried the sacred war bundle with its charms, and as they vanished into the forest each man followed close on the heels of the last.

"The English come to burn Itseyi," Nanyehi said. "We go to meet them on the way." Taking up her weapons, she nodded at the two pieces of cane and the belts and pouches on the floor mat. "For you. Come."

The bags held parched corn, and the hollow canes were filled with water. Bewildered, afraid, yet spellbound, Jamesina and Attercap found themselves swept into the dreamlike silence of a morning mist. They followed behind Nanyehi at the tail of one of the five war parties that had crossed the mountains from Itsati, the Beloved Town. Each warrior trotted within a few paces of the man before him, and they made no more sound than a stirring of leaves in the still gloom. Their silence seemed to come less from a fear of the enemy's scouts than from a fierce singleness of mind. Their way led up steep slopes and down the tumbled, broken rock of deep ravines, but the warriors did not stop to eat or drink or rest. Leaving the path, they passed through the forest to the west of Itseyi, the British army's destination. After a mile or so Tsulu sent Attercap up a tall tree to see what he could see through the thinning mist, perhaps to look for a landmark or telltale red coats. Tsulu did not say, and Jamesina and Attercap could not guess which. They had no idea how many miles lay between Itseyi and Fort Prince George.

At the side of a narrow stream running off to the south, Tsulu once again sent Attercap up the nearest tall tree. "Nothing," he reported quietly when he came down again. "Only a shallow valley, all bushes. It looks like a thicket wide and long as a lake."

Tsulu gave a nod, and the line of warriors turned and followed him northward through the trees in the direction of the great thicket. Nanyehi did not stir until they were out of sight. Then she motioned for Jamesina and Attercap to follow, and turned to wade the shallow stream and hurry on to the east. The way was hard and hilly, with deep hollows and dark, tangled underbrush. Twice she climbed trees herself to make sure of her way. At last, she brought them to the crest of a long, thinly wooded slope. From the shelter of a clump of laurels, she pointed down through the wisps of mist to a column of red-coated soldiers marching westward far below.

Red-coated men in kilts.

"Highlanders!" Jamesina began to tremble.

"You do not wish to see this war," Nanyehi warned.

"Stay here until all pass. Then follow back the way they come. To Fort Prince George."

Neither Jamesina nor Attercap could take their eyes from the endless line of Highlanders marching two abreast. When they did turn, Nanyehi had vanished.

Attercap stood staring. "Like the Nunnehi," he whispered.

Jamesina looked at him blankly.

"A sort of elvish spirit they tell of," he said, and shook his head as if to clear it.

Obediently, they sat down beneath the laurels to watch and wait. The column of marching men, glimpsed now and then, seemed to take forever to go by. At last, Attercap stirred and sat up straighter. "There—look below!"

The mist had thinned across the hillside, and one clear patch below had widened. A company of blue-coated Royal Americans had been followed by a straggle of militia in hunting shirts and moccasin boots. These were passing out of sight in turn, to be followed by a heavily laden pack train.

"Powder and shot." Attercap pointed to the wooden kegs and ammunition boxes that burdened the horses and mules. "The path is too rough and narrow for wagons. Come. They'll be past soon."

Jamesina pulled out the feathers braided in her hair. "Yours, too," she warned, "or they'll take us for Cherokees." They angled down to strike the track back to Fort Prince George near the rear of the pack train.

Some two hundred yards behind them three Highlanders climbed up out of the trees further along that same thinly wooded slope, to spy out the way the rangers had taken. In the thinning mist, they seemed almost *Nunnehi* themselves, half visible, their coats a faded, bloodless red.

Kenneth Mackenzie raised his arm to point.

29

A KILTED QUARTERMASTER SERGEANT STRIDING ALONG the line of pack animals, urging their leaders on, was first to see the two ragged figures step out of the mist. Startled, he drew and raised his pistol, only to lower it at Jamesina's cry.

"Na loisg oirnn. 'Se cairdean a tha unnainn! Inag Nic Coinnich agus Gilleasbuig Gordon a' dèanamh air Dun Prionnsa Sheòras. Na loisg oirnn! Do not shoot!"

Amazed, but in too great haste to stop for curiosity, he waved them back along the line.

As the last mule clip-clopped past, a straggling line of men and women came in sight, none in uniform, some carrying packs upon their backs, some not. As Jamesina stepped onto the path, she saw a tall, young man well out in front of the others stop in astonishment, to stand rooted in the middle of the track.

"Jamesina?"

Jamesina stumbled, and caught herself.

He was Dougal Macrae of Grudidh!

* * *

When they had recovered a little from their amazement, they sat down by the wayside with Attercap, and Dougal explained how he came to be there. Once recovered from the blow that felled him on the Gairloch shore, he had gone in search of the spiriters' ship. With money, letters of introduction, and a blessing from Old Rorie Mackenzie, he walked the rugged, ragged Highland coast southward, hearing here and there of sightings, until he found a fishing-boat captain who had seen her name. When he came to Glasgow and Port Glasgow, so many months had passed that he heard all the tale of the *Sparrowhawk*'s former captain, the greedy Lumsden, and the ship's unhappy voyage to Virginia. He had set sail for the colony himself, and walked the length of the wide James River in search of Jamesina. In Richmond, at Justice and Mrs. Moon's dinner table, he sat next to Royal—Prince Diai Boukari, who was soon to sail for England—and heard that Justice Moon's own search for Jamesina had led to the discovery of the Biggses' burnt-out cabin, and tell-tale signs of Cherokees. News of the army expedition to the Cherokee towns had drawn Dougal on to Charles Town, and then to the army rendezvous at Congarees.

"The Indian towns—the killing and burning . . ." He shook his head, and could not finish. "I feared I would find you too late."

"I should have known you would come." Jamesina, who sat between the two young men at the roadside, spoke with a gasp of shaky laughter. "I should have! But—did you say the troops were from the 77th Highlanders? 'Tis a strange world! The 77th was Kenneth and Donald and Davie's regiment."

"Aye, Colonel Montgomery and part of the 77th

were sent here from Canada. But—*'was'?*" Dougal gave her a puzzled look, and then a startled one. "Of course, you cannot know! Their letters were delayed for months. They came in a packet all together, after you were stolen from us. Whatever your 'seeing' meant, it was not that they were dead. They are here. Ahead. Not a mile up the line."

Jamesina stared at him in disbelief and then quickly, at the sound of a distant shot, up the forest track.

That first shot was followed by a ragged volley, and after it a steady crackle of distant gunfire like the crackling of a blaze in brushwood.

The great thicket lay spread like a net to catch fishes, too wide to go easily around, too still to seem a threat. As the mist that had filled it was banished by bright sunshine, it waited for the white men. Rangers scouted the way in, and were swallowed up in surprise. At the sound of shots and war whoops and wild yells, sixteen hundred infantrymen, militiamen, and grenadiers advanced and charged. In that dense thicket, the two invisible armies battled for upward of an hour.

And then it was over. The Cherokees and their dead and wounded vanished. The British lost only twenty men, but so many hundreds were wounded that the column of those limping or being carried back to the fort and the settlements far beyond was stretched out for half a mile, with the other troops marching before and behind.

Jamesina stood beside the wide-trampled path, eagerly searching each dusty, sweat-streaked face as the first Highlanders swung past behind the colonials. She saw a Mackenzie or two she knew—redheaded Robbie Mackenzie of Gairloch, for one—but no Kenneth or

Donald or Davie. They came in the column of wounded. Donald and Davie carried a shirtsleeved Kenneth on a litter rigged from two rough poles and his own plaid. His red coat served for a cover. Donald's head was bandaged. He staggered, and almost dropped the litter's poles when he saw the girl, so eerily familiar and strangely tall, who came flying down the ragged column toward him.

For all four, their astonishment was as deep as their delight. Attercap and Dougal took charge of the litter, and the four Mackenzies went hand in hand for most of the way to Fort Prince George. On the long march to Charles Town, too, Jamesina walked with her brothers, despite the frowns of the surgeon and regimental officers. She refused to be parted from them.

Though the Lower towns of the Cherokee were destroyed, the English settlements between the fort and Charles Town blamed Colonel Montgomery for not pushing further, to destroy the rest. The colonel, under orders to return his troops quickly to Albany and on to Canada, was scornful. "I have just burnt a dozen towns sweeter and cleaner than these, and killed some hundreds of men. If these colonials wish to steal Indian lands, I say let them see to their safety themselves."

Three ships rode at anchor in Charles Town harbor, waiting to carry the Highland and Royal American troops to New York—Donald and Davie among them—for their return to Canada. Kenneth Mackenzie, badly lamed by his wound, was taken aboard the first, the *Callisto*, and Jamesina and Dougal were allowed to go with him. From New York they were to sail for home. Attercap—Archie, now, for three months of Cherokee and Carolina food had left him no longer thin and spider-legged—could have gone with them, but did not.

Standing on the wharf with Jamesina, he looked from her to Donald, Davie, and Dougal as they helped Kenneth to board, and took a deep breath. "Ye're deep-rooted, lass. 'Tis why ye wilted so on the *Sparrowhawk*, from being snatched up so cruelly. But my roots were withered away already. I had no one and nowhere left to me. Ye'll think it queer, but in a month or two, if all is quiet here, I mean to return to Itsati. It will be safe enough, I think, behind its mountains."

Jamesina stood at the *Callisto*'s rail and watched the straight figure standing at the end of the wharf until the ships had sailed so far that she could not make him out. It was then, as the land fell away, that she began to understand, a little. She felt, almost with a pang, as if a great door were closing slowly behind her.

She was returning home, and happily.

But the far side of the sea would always be a bright shadow at the back of her mind.

Author's Note

The spiriters of the eighteenth century stole thousands of children to sell into bondage in America, most of them from the towns and surrounding countryside of Aberdeen, Bristol, and London. The tale Attercap recounts in Chapter 7, of the stolen boy who returned as a grown man to Aberdeen to expose the trade and its organizers, is true. His name was Peter Williamson.

The Nanyehi of my story is based upon the historical Nanyehi, who after a later marriage to an English trader was known as Nancy Ward. She was a friend to the colonists, and later the Americans, into her old age. Royal's story was inspired in part by the true history of Olaudah Equiano, a Fulani African prince sold into slavery, whose letter in Arabic describing his predicament came into the right hands. Freed, Equiano was taken to England, and returned in time to Africa. Fortune was not so kind to the Cherokees. In 1761, a year after Colonel Montgomery's troops sailed from Charlestown, the colonists' complaints brought a second British army to South Carolina, and the Middle towns of the Cherokee were destroyed. Itsati and the other Overhill towns remained safe beyond their mountains—but only for a time.